road to true north

SARAH HOLDING

road to true north
published by Firehorse Enterprises Ltd

ISBN: 978-1916307094
Copyright © Sarah Holding 2025

Printed by IngramSpark and KDP.
CIP Data: A catalogue record for this book
is available from the British Library.

Sarah Holding asserts her moral right to be identified
as the author of this book.

Cover image produced by the author.
Map illustration produced in ArcGIS by Ray Holding.
Typeset in Arno Pro.

road to
true north

SARAH HOLDING

FIREHORSE

SARAH HOLDING is also the author of the following titles:

SeaBEAN, the trilogy
'An interesting way of introducing young people to environmental issues'

CHAMELEON
'Does it have to cost the Earth to find out who we really are?'

blackloop
'Stranger Things' meets 'The Breakfast Club'

How to Write a Poem
and some other poems

**SCAN FOR
MORE INFO:**

acknowledgements

This novel was inspired by a road trip I took with my family around Iceland in the summer of 2015, and the first draft was written during a month-long writers' residency I attended at Arteles Creative Centre in Finland in November 2022.

Editorial advice and brainstorming partners are both a welcome and necessary part of the writing process, and I would particularly like to thank Kristi Dick, Lucy Dawes Durneen and Claire Corbett for their invaluable input.

No book can find its way into the world without being road-tested by expert readers, and in this case I am truly grateful to our dear friends Halldóra Hreggviðsdóttir and Matthildur Elmarsdóttir for their help in adjusting various Icelandic terms as well as cultural, meteorological and topographical aspects of the story.

Finally, thanks go to my family, who having undertaken a similar (albeit less eventful) road trip were uniquely able to give feedback and help shape the narrative. As always, my husband Eric helped me tease out the parts of the story that needed more time and space. Thank you darling; the novel is all the better for it.

I am dedicating this novel to fathers and sons everywhere, and in particular to our two dads, Bob and Chris, both of whom passed away while I was working on *Road to True North*.

Iceland

Þingvellir
reykjavík
geldingadalir
route 1
north american plate
eurasian plate

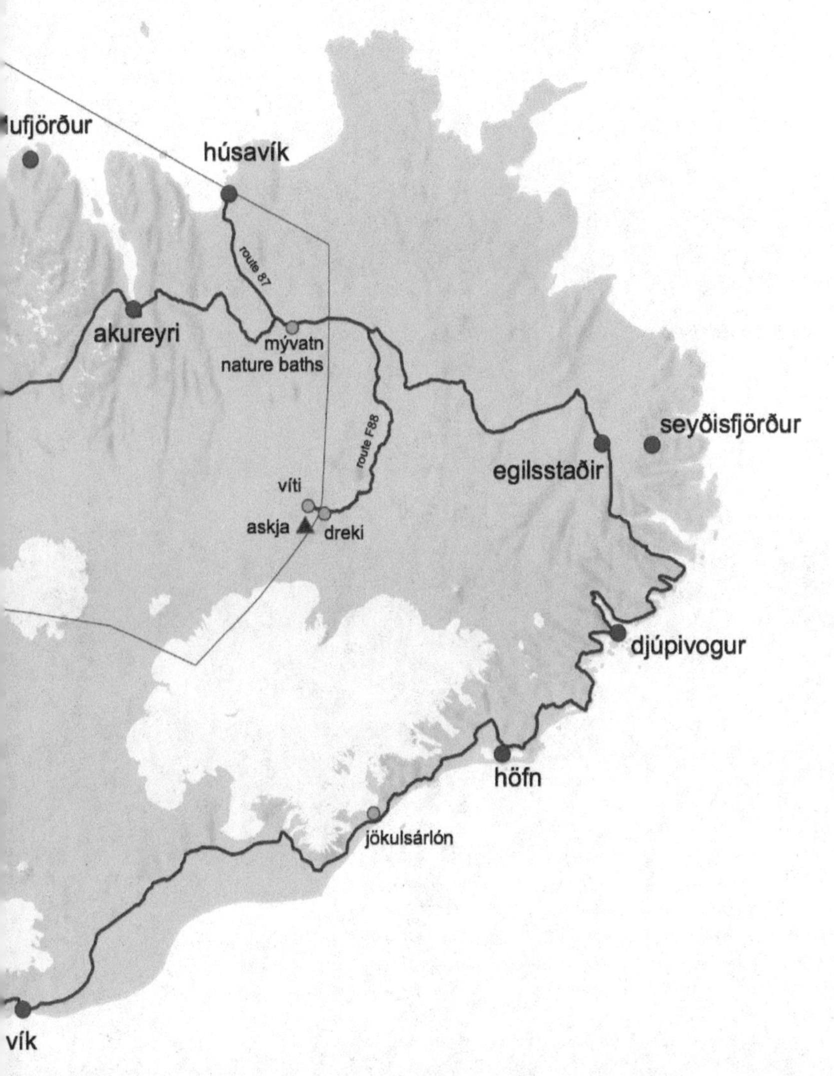

ufjörður
húsavík
route 87
akureyri
mývatn
nature baths
route F88
seyðisfjörður
egilsstaðir
víti
askja
dreki
djúpivogur
höfn
jökulsárlón
vík

Of all the places in the world, why had his father brought him to this desolate place? Olly stared glumly out of the window at the lumpen grey lava fields below, snow trapped in deep crevices, puffs of steam exhaling here and there. For a few seconds before they made abrupt contact with dark tarmac, Olly felt like the plane was a stone skimming over slowly undulating waves. In the long braking roar that followed, Olly took a deep breath and sighed. Then he felt the landing gear touch down on the runway and the captain's gravelly voice announced, 'Welcome to Iceland'.

Olly thought about all the places his father had been sent over the years to photograph aberrations in the earth's crust: the Rift Valley in Tanzania, Iguazu Falls in South America, twisted rock formations off the coast of Papua New Guinea. When he was little, Olly had been in awe of these tours of duty to exotic places, always eager to hear his father's crazy stories when he returned home to their flat in Kilburn. But now that he was finally accompanying his father on a work trip, it already seemed dull and disappointing. Not that he'd had much choice in the matter; it was a blatant act of parental coercion: *You're coming with me and that's final.* He had no idea how he was going to survive the next two weeks.

Sean leaned across the empty seat between them and nudged his son's elbow.

'Right Mr Midas, get your skates on. And let's not forget anything.'

Sean watched as his son, moving at a glacial pace, unbuckled himself and rooted around in the seat pocket to retrieve his headphones and a packet of gum. Locks of greasy black hair obscured most of his face except his set jawline, where Olly sported a crop of acne and a sparse adolescent beard. With great reluctance Olly dragged on his parka and Sean inwardly rolled his eyes when he caught sight of the red target sprayed on the back of the coat and was reminded of all the hoo-ha it had caused.

Feeling tetchy and already in need of a stiff drink, Sean stood up, stretched, zipped up his thick thermal coat, and opened the overhead locker. Olly's scruffy backpack, studded with button badges from all the gigs he'd been to, promptly tumbled down and landed on the empty seat between them.

'Lucky that wasn't my camera bag!' Sean muttered through gritted teeth. His son just shrugged and hoisted the backpack over his shoulder.

As if responding to the turbulence on the approach to Keflavik airport, Olly's stomach did a belated lurch, which he realised was actually hunger. He'd refused his mother's offer to make him scrambled eggs before they left the flat, protesting that it was 'far too early' to eat, and had made do later with a bag of crisps at the airport. Contrary to expectations, instead of heading straight for the bar once they were through security, his dad seemed to be restricting himself to a coffee and nicotine combo, which had the effect of enhancing Sean's frenetic work persona. Olly found this very out of character. At home, his dad was best known for falling asleep dead drunk on the sofa mid-way through a movie or pushing the trolley in a leisurely daze round Tesco in search of the aisle selling toothpaste or painkillers.

'Bollocks!' Olly muttered, as a sudden jolt of anxiety replaced his hunger pangs.

'What now?'

'Nothing.'

'Olly, what is it?'

He couldn't read his son's expression through the screen of hair, but from the way Olly was twisting his mouth and clicking out his finger joints, Sean knew something was up. He put a hand on Olly's shoulder and forced his torso round to face him, raising his eyebrows in a way that demanded a response.

'My meds. I left them on the kitchen table.'

'Shit. We'll get Mum to post them. They'll be here in a couple of days and…'

'But Dad…'

'What?' Sean barked, aware his voice had a steely edge that only happened when he was stone cold sober.

Other passengers were trying to edge past them, their polar outerwear chafing as they shepherded their carry-on cases towards the exit.

'Mum said… never mind, I'll tell you later.'

2

'He's asleep now,' Sean said, glancing over at the humped mass of grey duvet, rising and falling on the bed next to his. 'Are you sure this was a good idea, Tess?'

He took another swig from the miniature bottle of vodka he'd helped himself to from the mini bar and imagined his wife leaning against the velvet headboard in their double bed at home in Kilburn. He toyed with an alluring image of her dark hair coiled into a messy bun, her reading glasses magnifying her limpid green eyes and reflecting the glow from her laptop.

'It was your idea, remember?' she said, sighing. 'That what-shall-we-do-about-Olly conversation we had driving back from Jeanne's house after the August bank holiday? You thought it would take his mind off what happened, you know, get him to take an interest in something new.'

'Like what? Remind me.'

'Like… volcanoes, photography, I don't know Sean, big skies… "big nature" I think were your actual words. You were probably drunk when you said it and that's why you don't remember.'

Sean rolled his eyes.

'Look, it'll be OK once you get on the road. This is your chance "to be a good Dad", those were also your exact words as I recall.'

'Right.'

'Anything else you've forgotten?'

'Look, don't use that tone, Tess. It wasn't my fault our child forgot the one thing he really needed to bring with him.'

'I'm not using any tone, Sean. But you do have a habit of being a bit too casual about parenting, like most things. Especially when you've been drinking.'

'Oh come on, Tess, give me a break.'

'That's why you're there, sweetheart. To have a break.'

'Actually, this is a work trip. But with the additional responsibility of our son and his mental health issues. I've got quite a lot on my plate, so I'd hardly call it a break.'

'Well, you're not the only one. Listen, I need to get some sleep; I've got a lot on my mind, and I'm launching my new website tomorrow, or had you forgotten that too?'

'OK, Tess. I'll let you go. Night.'

Olly waited until his father had ended the call and closed the bathroom door before turning on the bedside light. He rummaged in his rucksack for his mobile and checked for messages. He longed to find a text waiting for him, but he knew the more he longed for one, the more unlikely it was that one would arrive. It had been ten days now since Sol's last message. The one with the picture of their tent on fire.

He listened as his dad cleaned his teeth with his special charcoal toothpaste, picturing globs of black spit landing in the white porcelain sink. In the silence that followed he could tell his father was now peering into the mirror to inspect the gap where a rotten incisor had recently fallen out; the latest excuse for his excessive drinking and drama over the past few weeks.

Olly was starting to feel too hot under the covers. He was still fully dressed, having pretended to fall asleep the moment he entered their hotel room and flung himself on the nearest bed, all to avoid some awkward father-to-son bedtime conversation that he felt was brewing. There wasn't enough time to take his clothes off now before his dad came out of the bathroom, so he just kicked off his trainers and the duvet and heaved himself onto his side. He hated that he didn't get to talk to his Mum just then. He hated the fact that he'd come on a trip with just his dad. He hated that they were here in this stupid hotel in this stupid country. But more than anything, he hated himself.

3

Waiting for his father to sign the paperwork for their rental vehicle, Olly stared across the car park through the drizzle at the row of shops opposite. He noticed one had a nice-looking guitar in the window. Picking up his backpack, he left his father's side and wandered out of the car hire place to take a closer look.

'Olly, wait, where are you going? We're almost done here,' Sean protested, but his son was already out of earshot.

Agitated, Sean clicked the ballpoint pen he was holding, the tendons in his neck pulsing against his skin. He repositioned the baseball cap on his head, using it to scratch an itch on his forehead, and watched as Olly peered through the window of the guitar shop, his chubby hand cupped against the glass.

'Will you be wanting snow studs? You'll need them if you're planning on driving into the Highlands at all on this trip,' the rental agent said.

'Go on then, you might as well,' Sean muttered as he watched his son dithering outside the shop.

'Sorry sir, was that a yes or a no?' the car rental employee asked, puzzled. Sean ignored him, too preoccupied with what his son was doing.

There was a poster in the shop window advertising an upcoming open mic event that caught Olly's eye, mainly because it was being held somewhere called The Midas Rooms. Olly took a picture of it with his phone, then glanced back across the parking lot and saw his dad was standing on the kerb, frowning impatiently. He sighed and walked back just as their rental vehicle pulled up; a glistening white

SUV with fat tyres and high wheel arches that sideways-on looked like his father's raised eyebrows.

'What do you think?'

'You're seriously gonna drive around Iceland in that ridiculous vehicle?'

'Guess I'll have to; you failed your test, remember?'

Olly sighed at the familiar dig.

'Only joking, Olly-Moo,' his father said, cuffing him lightly.

'Yeah, right.'

Sean strode round the SUV, opened up the back and lobbed their two suitcases into the boot. By force of habit, Olly opened the rear passenger door and started to climb in.

'Hey! I might be your designated driver but I'm not a sodding taxi. Sit in the front.'

Olly left his backpack on the back seat, slammed the door shut with as much force as he could muster and got in the front, making a big deal out of sliding the seat backwards, reclining it and adjusting the headrest. Everything was new and stiff.

'It stinks, Dad.'

'What does?'

'This car.' If she was here, Mum would be telling them how all the chemicals being emitted from the plastic dashboard and the vinyl seats were going to 'play havoc' with their immune systems or something. But Olly knew if he said something like that, it would have zero impact on his father.

'It'll wear off in the few days. Once I've filled up the ashtray.'

'There's a sticker right there that says no smoking, Dad. Can't you read?'

'The only stuff you need to be reading from now on is this map, Olly.' Sean leaned over to the back seat and grabbed a brand-new map of Iceland which he dumped in Olly's lap. 'That's your job. Navigation. Not nagging. If I wanted to be nagged, I'd have brought your mother.'

'Nice.'

'What was that?'

'Nothing.'

'OK, ready for the off?'

4

It started raining as soon as they turned onto Route One, which led northeast out of Reykjavík. Once he'd worked out there were very few turnings to their first destination – a place called Þingvellir – Olly stopped navigating and trained his eyes instead on the scarred surfaces of the brooding volcanic rock that started appearing as the city thinned out. The smooth black flank in the distance looked like a prehistoric sea creature he'd seen in a documentary at Sol's house, its head submerged but its long curving spine arching proud of the water. It was a nice outline. He imagined Sol drawing it as a single charcoal mark on a huge sheet of paper and let out a sigh.

The traffic in front was a solid flow of red tail lights clogging the highway. For a country with so few people, there were a lot of cars on the road, Olly decided. He watched as a skinny woman came out of her front door in Lycra jogging gear, started her Apple stopwatch, then set off running up the steep road past a group of tourists who were queuing in front of their hotel to get on a minibus with a 'Highland Adventures' decal on its side. On the outskirts of town, the colourful old timber and corrugated iron houses gave way to grey apartment blocks whose curtainless windows stared out bleakly at the monotonous landscape.

'Brought any good music to listen to?' his father asked, fiddling with the buttons on the radio and getting only static.

'Yeah, on my phone. But it's not your standard Classic FM stuff.'

'Better than driving the whole way in silence though, eh?'

Olly sighed and reached behind him to get his phone out of his backpack. He had made a pact with himself not to check for messages until they stopped for lunch. It was only half eleven.

Out of the corner of his eye Sean watched his son scroll through his phone, finally settling on an album with complicated burnt-looking artwork, and then without missing a beat, connected his phone to the car's sound system via Bluetooth, as if this sort of knowhow was hardwired into his eighteen-year-old brain. The opening chords were a menacing jangle, but the dirty bass line grew into a pleasing throb that aligned with Sean's heart rate, elevated by the strong coffee he'd drunk at breakfast. He tapped his fingers against the steering wheel to let Olly know he approved of his choice of soundtrack. But when he turned his head sideways to see if this had registered on Olly, Sean saw a tear rolling down his child's cheek.

Jesus. Tess had better have posted those meds this morning. He'd text her when they next stopped. Olly wasn't going to do too well without them, that much was clear.

5

'Time for a pitstop,' Sean announced, swinging off Route One into a newish-looking service station advertising electric charging points and hot dogs. The car's petrol gauge was still registering full, but he needed to pee and top up his caffeine and nicotine levels.

Olly rolled down the window, breathed in the damp air and shivered. He seemed to be the only person in Iceland without a down-filled all-weather coat to fend off the icy wind. Just his old blue parka with the ripped lining. It was Sol's idea to spray a red target on the back of it, which Olly's parents had been most unimpressed about, so he was quite attached to it. He watched as his father strode off towards the building and emerged a few minutes later clutching a hotdog in one hand and a steaming cup of espresso in the other.

'Here, I put ketchup on it for you,' Sean said, handing it over through the car window, 'The mustard looked pretty grim.'

Olly bit into the hotdog, licking his fingers as the ketchup oozed out of the paper napkin. As he chewed the soggy bread, he could hear his mother's voice telling him that they grind up pigs' lungs and intestines to make hotdog sausages. Anyway, it tasted good. Standing on a patch of grass beside the SUV, his dad knocked back the coffee, sucked the life out of a cigarette and then ground the butt into two dimensions under his walking boot. Olly rolled his eyes as his father then proceeded to do his annoying exercise routine – twisting in either direction to click out his spine and then doing a series of press-ups against the side of the SUV – which made the vehicle rock from side to side.

'We need to turn right in a mile or two to get to that place Thing-

Vellir,' Olly announced as Sean climbed back into the vehicle. His father gave a slight nod and revved the engine, the indicator ticking loudly as they pulled out of the service station.

A few miles later, Olly cleared his throat.

'You just missed the turning.'

'What turning?'

'The one I told you about.'

'Jesus, kiddo! Your navigation skills suck. Can't you tell me before the turning instead of afterwards, like any normal person. We'll save a hell of a lot of time and petrol that way.'

Sean swung the car into a lay-by, revved dramatically then lurched it back round to return to the intersection. Half a mile later he realised there was nothing coming out through the car speakers anymore and Olly was now listening to his doom-laden music via his headphones. Probably some kind of silent protest. Sean clenched his teeth and instantly regretted it as a sharp pain shot along his jaw.

6

A brown tourist sign for Þingvellir loomed into view and Sean pulled up outside the visitor centre. Olly wrestled with the laminated map, trying to fold it away, then gave up, crushing it against the windscreen so that he could swing his feet onto the dashboard to lace up his walking boots.

'You should treat maps with more respect; they're endangered species,' his father quipped as he got out of the vehicle, did ten more press-ups for good measure and then walked round to get his photography equipment out of the boot.

'Come on kiddo, I want to show you something. This is the best place in Iceland to really get your head around its awesome volcanic and seismic features.'

Sean strode off, tripod in hand, camera bag slung across his shoulder. Olly thought his Dad looked and sounded like a frustrated geography teacher as he followed him reluctantly along a boardwalk, sensing a lecture in the offing, which was going to be totally embarrassing, given all the tourists he'd seen getting off coaches.

They were walking between a weird gap in the rocks, which looked like two vertical cliffs facing each other, as if someone had cut a huge stack of pancakes in half.

'How about this Olly: right here is the only place in the world where you get to experience the North American plate and the Eurasian plate pulling apart from each other.'

Sean indicated the phenomenon with both arms outstretched and Olly pictured being ripped in two, which caused a slight wrench in his abdomen.

'And that's because the rest of this plate boundary is under the ocean, forming the Mid Atlantic Ridge,' his dad added over his shoulder, drawing a line in the air with his hand.

After ten minutes' walking, the gap widened out into a valley filled with a huge lake edged with ribbed rock that was hard to walk on.

'Come on Olly, let's keep moving. I want to get some shots from the other side.'

Sean pressed on towards an outcrop of rock where there was a tourist viewpoint.

'I say forget Hawaii or Indonesia or Japan, kiddo; Iceland is where it's at if you want to capture the most dramatic effects of volcanic activity! I always tell people my job is about capturing what's going on at the surface so we can picture what's really going on underneath.'

Olly nodded, not wanting to give his father too much encouragement, or the lecture could go on forever. To show willing, he took a couple of shots with his phone and decided to post them as a story on Instagram, casually tagging Sol. If Sol was deliberately ignoring his texts, this might be another way of getting a message through.

'Anyway, that's not the only reason Þingvellir is important to Icelanders. This is where you get your history kicks too, because one of the earliest parliaments in the world took place right here, over a thousand years ago. Back in 930 AD, the elders from all the remote Icelandic communities would have arrived here on horseback, where there was plenty of pastureland for their horses to graze on in a secure and protected valley, while they discussed the order of the day.'

'What does 'thing-fellir' mean?'

'Glad you asked, Mr Midas. Thing means assembly, and vellir means fields I believe. So, a place of gathering, if you will. And that's the biggest natural lake in the whole of Iceland over there.'

Olly had the feeling that his dad was going to spend the next two weeks pointing out all the biggest, longest, oldest, tallest, widest, deepest things this whole trip. This was just the beginning.

7

There was a sign up ahead that said *sundlaug* and Olly did a quick Google Translate on his phone. Swimming Pool.

Right on cue, his father asked, 'Fancy a quick dip?'

'In this weather? No thanks.'

'It'll be nice and warm, you'll see.'

Sean turned off the main road down a dirt track, the SUV hobbling over rocks and lurching from side to side. Round the next bend, a cloud of steam filled a small hollow beside a wooden hut.

Within seconds, his father had parked up, peeled off his clothes and plunged like an Olympic swimmer into the gleaming patch of sulphurous water.

'Did we bring towels?' Olly yelled into the steam when his father's head resurfaced.

'Nope. Just get in, it's great.'

Sean began crawling in earnest up and down the tiny pool. Olly rolled his eyes and unzipped his parka. He walked over to the wooden hut and found it was completely empty apart from a row of hooks and a bench. He undressed slowly and hung each item of clothing on one of the hooks, then dithered, shivering inside the hut, before emerging, podgy and sullen, in just his boxer shorts.

His father was languishing at the far end of the little pool, his curly hair now wet and flat against his scalp, one elbow draped casually along the edge.

'You're going in like that?'

'What does it look like?'

Sean watched as Olly stepped tentatively onto the metal ladder and lowered himself into the green water, his boxers billowing slightly as they became waterlogged. He reminded Sean of an oversized baby in a giant nappy.

The pool smelled like eggy farts and the water was scalding. Olly felt his stomach clench up as he pushed off and swam towards his father in a childish doggy paddle. His could tell his face was turning red from exertion, and it brought back a memory of the traumatic day aged six when he learned to swim at their local pool in Kilburn. Right after he'd done a tentative first width, his father took off the armbands and commanded him to do it again unaided. He remembered flailing around underwater with no idea how to reach the surface, swallowing a lungful of chlorine and then getting out just in time to throw up in the changing rooms. Keeping his mouth tightly shut Olly struggled to put the incident out of his mind and keep his chin above the murky water. When he reached the end where his father was, he wanted to grab onto the edge, but the sides of the pool were slimy and off-putting, so he had to tread water instead, panting for air.

'Not so bad is it, this Iceland malarkey?'

'Is this free or do we have to pay?' Olly gasped, pushing his wet hair out of his eyes.

'Nah, this is just one of the perks of the job!' Sean declared, gesturing to the vast mountainside behind them, the rocky inlet below them, the tufted grass and sheep. He'd come to the conclusion that people who were loaded – like their friend Anton for instance – could keep all their fancy five-star hotels and first-class air travel nonsense. This was Sean's idea of luxury: simple, remote, impromptu. Perfection.

Well, almost. A tumbler of vodka wouldn't go amiss right now. And if he was honest, he'd rather be on his own than with Olly. But better Olly than Anton, given the choice. If Anton was here, he'd be talking incessantly about his latest crypto exploits or his horse-riding lessons, or some equally dull topic that only Tess could manage to show an interest in.

Sean breathed in the sulphurous air and smiled as a vision of his perfect travel companion came to mind. It took him right back to the very first time he'd visited Iceland, years ago when he was still a student. He'd dropped his camera down an icy crevasse on the second day, but it hadn't mattered because he'd met a Danish girl called Mette and had fallen hopelessly in love.

8

'Why are we driving all the way around the edge of Iceland? Wouldn't it be much quicker to go across the middle?' Olly asked as they climbed into the car the following day.

'Well, if you un-scrunch that very expensive map I bought, you'll see that the whole of the middle of Iceland is a bleak, uncharted territory called The Highlands. It's like the Cairngorms in Scotland only colder and much more desolate. Best avoided in winter unless you fancy getting frostbite or getting lost in a white-out. Suffice to say, as with any glaciated wilderness, you better know what you're doing if you're going to venture into the middle of Iceland.'

Olly peered at the largely unmarked area of white and blue in the dead centre of the map, and noticed there were no proper roads, towns or even villages. It looked about as empty as he felt inside, and he had a momentary feeling of empathy for this strange, unknowable place.

Sean put the key in the ignition.

'Mum says your tablets will be here tomorrow. How are you feeling today, kiddo?'

'Why are you asking?' Olly gave him a sidelong glance.

'I'm just 'checking in', like Mum does.'

'Feels weird when you do it.'

'Really? May I ask why?' Sean raised his eyebrows to show he expected an answer.

'Dunno, it's just not your thing, that's all.'

'Well, I am your dad; I care about you just as much as Mum does.'

'Right.'

Olly fidgetted with the zip on his backpack, running it backwards and forwards, feeling the teeth zig-zagging together and apart, together and apart, metal biting onto metal. Already irked, Sean exhaled noisily, revved the engine and swung out of the hotel car park.

'Longish drive this morning to Vík. Hope you've got some more tunes lined up.'

His son made no effort to reply. Instead, he slunk lower in his seat and propped both socked feet on the dashboard. How do you get through to a teenager, Sean found himself wondering for the umpteenth time. What do you say to get them to switch out of this mute, barely monosyllabic gear and into something more expansive? He tried to picture himself at the same age, holidaying with his parents at their caravan in Dumfries with nothing but a cassette player for company. Maybe he'd acted just the same, always trying to creep back to his bunkbed or wander off round the caravan site on his own. Olly was the only son of an only son. Did that have something to do with it? His reluctance to talk, to share? As a child, Sean had always felt like an interloper in his parents' marriage, a spare part, a fly in the ointment.

Of course, in his own case, he dearly wanted to have more children with Tess, but it hadn't turned out that way. After Olly's difficult birth, Tess kept putting off trying to conceive their second, and by the time she agreed to try again, it seemed her body clock had decided it was too late. Sean suspected she was secretly glad but had never confronted her on the issue. Tess was always saying that she couldn't imagine loving another child the way she loved Olly. Suffocatingly, in his opinion. Always fussing, always trying to pre-empt disaster. Not that it had worked; she hadn't managed to avert the forgotten meds. Or the fiasco in the summer that had precipitated this whole trip. In a way, Tess was annoyingly like his own mother, doting on Olly and breathing down his neck all the time. How was he ever going to amount to anything in life if she kept him so close? Maybe if she'd let him fend for himself a bit more, he would have passed his exams and got into uni. Maybe if she'd let him figure things out on his own, Olly would have a better sense of his own identity by now and wouldn't have got mixed up in... well, all that trouble. Forget being tied to her apron strings, Sean was convinced Tess was practically swaddling Olly to death.

Before they'd left London, he'd made up his mind to give Olly more space on this trip, to let him grow up a bit, find his own way, but now that they were here in Iceland, he had no idea how to adopt this approach to parenting. Maybe he should start by asking fewer questions and instead open up a bit more about himself. Maybe that would encourage Olly to do the same – when he felt ready. But as he tried to think of something from his past to reveal to his child, something that would present himself in a more vulnerable light and less of the confident, capable father-figure, he cringed with embarrassment. Maybe even he wasn't ready for that kind of conversation. Not without a couple of drinks, anyhow. Nevertheless, Sean was painfully aware of a yawning gap between them and the lack of anything coherent to fill it with, so as he stared at the sleek black road spiked at intervals with yellow posts on either side, he started counting them under his breath. One, two, three... they pulsed by at the same rate his heart beat out its own fractious rhythm.

'What are you counting?' Olly asked after a while, his tone gruff and awkward.

'The yellow posts.'

'Why do they put them all along every road in Iceland?'

'So that when it snows you can still tell where the road is.'

'Does it snow a lot here?'

'In the Highlands, yeah, not so much along the coast.'

'That bit in the middle, you mean? What's there, exactly?'

'You name it: volcanoes, glaciers, white water rivers, and barely any sign of human or even animal life. Just vast expanses of sky and rock and the elements. It's a photographers' paradise.'

'So why aren't we going, Dad?'

'Your mother made me promise I wouldn't take you on any roads that aren't covered in tarmac or any place where you're supposed to register first before you go there.'

'Register?'

'Yes, with the Icelandic authorities. You register your intention to travel into the Highlands in advance, via a special government website, so they know where to look if you get lost. You tell them who's going, what route you'll be taking, and then check off a long list of things you need to take with you, because there are no petrol stations, shops, or places to stay for hundreds of miles.'

'Sounds more like the Sahara.'

'Well, it is a desert of sorts. An arctic one.'

'But we won't get any snow where we're going?'

'Probably not,' Sean said, rubbing his chin.

'What about the northern lights? We're going to see those, right?'

'Not that likely at this time of year, to be honest. The sky needs to be dark and perfectly clear to see them.'

'Shame. But we will get to see a volcano erupting, right? Surely that happens all the time in Iceland?'

'As far as I know, there are none that are active right now, sorry kiddo.'

Olly sighed. He gazed up at the clouds and thought about the shimmering technicolour panoramas he'd seen on all the Icelandic websites his mum had shown him when she was trying to soften the blow after his Dad had bellowed 'Look son, you're coming on this trip whether you like it or not'. Their usual good cop, bad cop routine. Except weirdly on that occasion, neither of them had gone full-on forensic about what happened that night. Nor had they asked who Sol was or how they'd met each other. Olly got the sense that they strongly disapproved of the relationship and were both hoping this trip would cure him of his so-called obsession with Sol. Not that they'd ever used the word 'obsession' to his face, but he'd heard his mother on the phone to Auntie Jeanne refer to Sol in that way. It was none of their business and he had no intention of telling his parents what he'd been going through lately. His mum would just get upset and his dad would get angry as hell, especially if he was blind drunk at the time.

'So basically, all that northern lights stuff is just cynical marketing bullshit? I bet the sky never goes vivid green or red,' Olly observed flatly, 'I bet it's always this grey and boring.'

His father didn't reply. Olly tried to look for a gap in the clouds, a tiny patch of blue where his mind could escape to, somewhere far away from his oppressive low mood. But rain was already blurring the windscreen, the first drops joining together and sliding in diagonal lines towards the corners. As his Dad flicked on the windscreen wiper which swept away the rain in one big semi-circular motion, Olly closed his eyes and listened instead to the repetitive sound of the rubber blade as it flexed back and forth against the glass. He tapped out a syncopated counter-rhythm on his thigh, nodding his head in time, hearing a loud, dissonant chord cutting through it.

Clocking his son's actions, Sean started to drum his fingers on the steering wheel in response. There was a brief moment when they synced up and Olly made a sound like he was about to laugh, but instead he sneezed, and the connection was gone.

9

Black sand stretched before them as if a layer of ash and soot covered the entire beach. The sky was an ominous dark grey, turning paler at the horizon as the drab afternoon light ebbed away. Sean stared at the water's edge, where the crashing white waves and retreating foam made the whole scene look like a film shot in black and white where the contrast had been boosted to enhance the monochromatic effect. The red target on the back of Olly's parka was the only colour in the entire scene, and the more Sean thought about it, the more he regarded it as evidence of his son's growing persecution complex. They'd come to Vík mainly so Sean could get some shots of the towering basalt cliffs for a client. His boss said they were urgent, but instead of doing what David asked, Sean felt compelled to face in the other direction and shoot this lonely, hunched teenager outlined against the sky, as he faced the oncoming waves.

Olly stooped to pick up a smooth, dark pebble. It felt nice to hold, cool and soothing. He shoved it in his pocket and picked up another, flatter one, then walked closer to the sea. On a calm day Olly knew he could make a stone like this skim the surface seven or eight times, each skip half the distance of the last one, in a perfect harmonic sequence. But the waves were choppy, and the pebble only skipped twice before sinking, leaving Olly's imagination to complete its intended arc, like mapping out a new chord sequence in his mind.

He was missing his guitar. Why hadn't he brought it with him? Mum had even suggested it, but without an amp and his effects pedals, what was the point? The strings sounded thin and unexpressive without those dirty distortions, the chords too clean and hopeful. Like music by Coldplay. He hated their thin, nasal sound, their pathetic lyrics. His mother was always on at him to write some of songs of his own, but without Sol to bounce ideas off it was too difficult. He longed to write something good that he could play to Sol when he got back. Something dark and brooding like this beach. But he didn't have the energy somehow. Or the self-belief.

He knelt down and worked both hands into the black sand, as if they were two flounders seeking refuge beneath the seabed from a predator. When he pulled them back out, it looked like he was wearing thick black gloves, and for a brief moment as setting sun broke through the clouds, and a pale-yellow spike caught the fine grains of sand, his hands sparkled as though they were covered with glitter. Olly remembered that he'd once tipped a whole pot of gold glitter on the floor in their flat when he was a toddler. With gluey hands, he'd crawled right through it, and transferred gold glitter to door handles, taps, the toilet seat – everything he touched – for days afterwards, despite his mother's best efforts to remove the stuff. It became a family joke and the source of Olly's stupid nickname, Mr Midas, which at some point had mutated into Midas-Moo, and more recently, Olly-Moo. To be honest, it felt more like a curse than a nickname because, unlike the myth, it seemed that nothing Olly touched ever turned to gold. Still, he'd rather be called any of those names than his dad's current favourite, 'Kiddo', which drove him mad. He didn't need to be constantly reminded that he was a stupid adolescent who'd failed to get the grades he needed to get into university – failed to 'keep his shit together' was how Dad put it – or in his mother's eyes, he'd failed to 'live up to his potential'. Of course she hadn't said it to his face, it was just something else he'd heard her whispering on the phone to Auntie Jeanne, when she rang to ask her what she should do with a 'semi-comatose' child. Even his godmother seemed at a loss, and the only thing she'd come up with was getting him a ticket to that lame music festival that only sixteen-year-olds went to. Now, because it was Jeanne's idea, his Mum had fallen out with her, but it wasn't her fault what happened. It wasn't anyone's fault but Olly's. He blamed himself for agreeing to go, blamed himself for what happened to him and Sol, and now he only had himself to blame for being here on this pointless trip around Iceland.

He tried to scrape the black sand off his palms, but it was sticky with salt, and he had no choice but to go down to the water's edge and rinse it off.

Sean watched as his son trudged even closer to the incoming waves and wondered what he was about to do. Surely he wasn't about to walk into the sea, not after his pathetic show of unwillingness yesterday at the little swimming pool they'd found? What was all that about, Sean wondered, he can't seriously be scared of a bit of warm water on top of being down in the dumps? He thought about calling out to Olly, but the wind was blowing in the opposite direction, and he wouldn't be able to hear. What did he want to tell him anyway? Watch out! Don't get wet! Time to go! Sean realised how many of the verbal statements he directed at Olly were actually abrupt commands. Tess was always telling him it was important for children to have other kinds of interactions and conversations with their parents. That as a parent, he should focus more on finding things to talk about rather than issuing instructions. But what was there to say?

The sea invaded Olly's walking boots and made his socks wet. He could feel the icy water sloshing between his toes. At least his hands, though cold and red, were now free of black sand. He shoved them deep in the pockets of his parka and made his way back up the beach to where his father had planted the tripod.

'How was the water?' Sean enquired, his eye glued to the viewfinder of his camera as he rattled off a volley of shots.

'Like, freezing. I'm not swimming in it, if that's what you're thinking.'

Sean laughed, but it came out a bit forced, a bit sarcastic.

'Maybe next time,' he mumbled.

10

'Some of them take as long as five years to melt,' Olly heard the woman in the puffy red tour guide coat say to another member of their group, as she gestured to the immense slabs of translucent turquoise-blue ice floating in the lagoon. She reached over the side of the boat and scooped up a beaker of water flecked with volcanic ash.

'Anyone want to taste water that's been trapped inside an iceberg for a thousand years? Go on, it's not going to hurt you. In fact, some Icelanders believe it's very rejuvenating because of all the minerals dissolved in it.'

There was a ripple of laughter among the tourists behind him, and Olly wondered what they found funny about the woman's invitation. Embarrassed at being invited to drink a substance of questionable origin maybe, or that sudden reference to a timeline that made them feel weirdly short-lived and insignificant? He knew Sol would have taken a sip, but somehow Olly couldn't bring himself to reach for the beaker. He thought it was because it reminded him of chemistry labs; the millilitre graduations printed in red on the side gave him the vague sense it might contain something toxic. He half expected his dad to say something annoying and witty to break the socially awkward silence, then remembered he wasn't there.

'I've got some things to do this morning, Olly-Moo,' his father had announced over breakfast, 'But don't worry, I've booked you onto a tour round Jökulsarlon.'

'What the hell's that?'

'Cheer up! You'll like it. It's very… blue.'

'Is that supposed to be a joke?'

'Come on, I'm not that mean. You might see a few seals too, if you're lucky.'

'So, it's like an aquarium?'

'Not exactly; it's a glacial lagoon that started forming in the 1930s. It's the deepest water in Iceland, in fact.'

The deepest. Olly took in this information as he tucked into his third croissant. He pictured the bottom of the lagoon, darker and colder than the sea yesterday, and shivered.

'Why aren't you coming, Dad?'

'I already told you; I've got a boring work issue to sort out for David. Plus, I need to phone a dentist. My missing tooth is killing me.'

'How can a missing tooth hurt?' Olly asked, picturing the dark cavity in his father's mouth like a miniature version of the lagoon.

'Must have got infected or something. Anyway, I need to get it sorted out.'

'OK, whatever.'

'So, I'll drop you off in the car park. The tour's at 11.'

Olly looked at his watch. It was now midday and his tummy was already rumbling. They were only halfway through the boat trip but he'd seen enough floating turquoise icebergs for now. He rummaged in his backpack for something to snack on and saw there was a notification on his phone. His heart pounding, Olly pulled it out and stared at the lockscreen.

Hi sweetie, how's it going? Hope you're having fun
and that Dad is behaving himself. Mum xx

He sighed and returned the phone to his backpack, fervently wishing it had been from Sol. More to the point, longing for those two kisses to be from Sol. Why hadn't they kissed or made out properly that night? Why hadn't they realised what was happening before it was too late? How come Sol got arrested and not Olly? He'd tried to apologise a million times for what happened, but there are things you can't control, things that can't be helped, things that create a massive, aching void that can't be filled.

Mum still had no idea what went on that night. Nor had Dad. He'd arrived at the police station around 3am with a face that hadn't decided whether to be angry or pleased to see his son. A few days afterwards, while Olly was worried sick about whether Sol would be sent to prison, his parents hatched this ridiculous plan to punish their child by sending him to Iceland. Of course they hadn't put it quite like that. Dad had made some long-winded speech about how Iceland was going to solve everything.

As if Iceland could fill this gaping hole inside him.

'Are you OK, sir?' the tour guide asked, and Olly realised with a start that she was speaking to him. He was pretty sure no one had ever called him 'sir' before. It made him feel a bit more grown up and he unhunched his shoulders. She was still holding the beaker of water.

'I'm fine. Just a bit… thirsty. Is it OK if I drink the water?'

'Sure, go right ahead,' she said, handing it to him.

Olly put the beaker to his lips, imagining it was one of his Mum's weird-tasting home remedies, or that pink liquid his dad drank to ease his stomach after a drinking binge. Knocking it back in one gulp, he was surprised to find it was neither: it was something so pure and soothing that when it slid down his throat, it made him feel utterly alive. He found himself uttering a silent prayer to the ancient Icelandic gods that this thousand-year-old glacier water would cure everything that was wrong with his life.

11

Sean drove like a lunatic the whole way to Höfn with a bottle of vodka in his lap. The scenery was utterly spectacular, but he didn't want to slow down and enjoy it at a leisurely place, or even photograph it, mainly because the pain had spread along his jaw and was now lurking in his left cheekbone. He nearly veered off the road multiple times, distracted by an intoxicating series of mental images the vodka was conjuring up: Mette, her long hair. Her even longer legs. The way she constantly twined and untwined them. He wondered, not for the first time, whether it was a sign he'd failed to notice, a sign that she felt uncomfortable when she was with him.

What had their relationship meant to her? What had it meant to him? Even though he was in love with her, when Mette said she wanted to split up with him, it was almost a relief to be free from the confines of his first serious relationship and to have his whole twenties ahead of him. When he heard she was dating this Irish guy, Sean felt only mildly jealous at the thought of her lying beside some pasty bloke reciting Yeats to her every night. It was nothing compared to Anton's jealous reaction twenty years ago when he banged on Tess's door that memorable January evening. Sean answered the door in his underpants and before he knew what was happening, Anton had given him a black eye to let him know precisely what a jilted lover's jealousy ought to feel like.

As far as Sean knew, Anton had never had another long-term relationship in the twenty years since losing Tess. He might have turned up at their wedding unannounced and made a speech about no hard feelings, but nevertheless, Anton still showed up at their flat more often than Sean would have liked, to have what he called 'a little catch-up' with Tess. Did that make Sean jealous? He was never sure. Maybe. It always put him slightly on edge, and he would often leave Anton regaling Tess with his exploits, then lie in bed upstairs wondering whether it had been a smart move or not.

Funnily enough, the only time Sean actually felt wildly jealous was seeing Tess snuggled up with Olly on the sofa when he came home drunk and got the feeling they'd been conspiring against him. Come to think of it, that sounded more like paranoia than jealousy. Maybe he was jealous of their closeness, even if it wasn't something he wanted for himself. What he wanted was an easy life, an easygoing kid, and a beautiful wife who was a little more laid back and who didn't maintain a platonic relationship with her ex, Anton Keeler.

'What the hell did Tess mean about having a lot on her mind?' he yelled angrily to himself, as he braked suddenly, skidding on the loose gravel at the edge of the road, before pulling into a small parking lot next to the ocean to have another swig or two of vodka. Sean glanced at his watch, as if checking up on himself. It was just after midday; no shame in that.

Sitting on the seawall, the Icelandic spirits slipped down easily, creating a pleasant warm prickle under his skin that reached almost to his jaw and cheek after several long gulps.

He rested his gaze on the skerries marooned out to sea, at the craggy white lighthouse that looked very much like Sean's missing incisor. He ran his tongue over the gap in his mouth, as if exploring its absence would ease the pain. Out of the corner of his eye, he noticed a dog running on the sand, its owner a tall willowy figure, whose long blonde hair whipped around her head like seagrass. Like Mette's. He wondered what Mette was doing right now, where in the world she was living, if she was still with the pasty Irishman. If she ever thought about her relationship with Sean. If she'd ever really loved him. At least he was fairly sure Tess loved him. Why else would she have put up with him for so long?

Speak of the devil; his pocket buzzed. Sean pulled out his phone and glanced at the notification.

'Shit! Forgot to call the office,' he groaned as he picked up, 'Hello?'

'Sean? Don't tell me there was no signal this time.'

'Hey David, no, just a few logistical hitches,' he slurred.

'Such as? You were supposed to send me those shots of Vík by 9am this morning.'

'Yeah, I know, but they came out pretty dark, I'm gonna have to do some work on them.'

'OK, I'll buy you some time and tell the client they'll have them by Friday. Sean, are you listening? Don't let me down.'

'Sure thing. Friday.'

His boss hung up just as the blonde woman with the dog walked past him.

'Hæ,' she said, smiling, 'Nice spot for a drinking session.'

Sean had no idea whether it was intended as a sarcastic comment or a friendly compliment.

'Yeah,' he replied lamely and half smiled, hoping she wouldn't notice his missing tooth.

12

'Had enough to eat?'

Olly nodded, swallowed his last mouthful of salad and then pushed his plate aside without tearing his gaze away from the football game on the screen at the back of the restaurant. He wasn't the slightest bit interested in football, let alone this Icelandic league match, but it saved him from having to sit opposite his father and smell his boozy breath or look at his bloodshot eyes.

'Shall we Facetime your mum when we get back to our room?'

'No need; I talked to her earlier.'

'Oh? What did she have to say?'

'She's going camping in the New Forest at the weekend.'

'Really? Who with?'

'She didn't say. Friends, I s'pose.'

Sean studied his son's expression to see if there was anything he wasn't letting on about this phone conversation with his wife, but Olly just looked bored underneath his overgrown fringe.

'You need a haircut, kiddo.'

'You need to stop drinking.'

In the pause that followed his curt comeback, Olly felt a little rush of adrenaline creep up his neck as he realised he'd actually said out loud what he'd been wanting to say all day, and especially all through dinner. He gave Sol an imaginary high five and tried hard not to smirk.

'Look, cut me some slack, OK? Until I get to see a dentist, vodka is the best thing for pain relief,' his dad responded haughtily. But when he stood to leave the table, he stumbled backwards and almost lost his balance.

Olly rolled his eyes, picked up his glass and drank the last of his mineral water. He hated having to deal with his dad's feeble excuses and shady behaviour on his own. Mum was much better at handling it than him. He was dreading how much worse this was going to get, the further round Iceland they drove. Luckily the opportunities to obtain alcohol were pretty limited in Iceland, so it could have been a lot worse. Olly had already taken the precaution of checking Google Maps to see how many vínbúðin they'd need to avoid in the remote northeast of the country where they were headed, but he knew from bitter past experience how devious and determined his dad was where drink was concerned.

13

Olly lay awake staring at the dark sliver of night sky between the curtains in their hotel room, listening to his father snoring loudly on the other bed, his mouth wide open, breathing like a rasping bulldog.

A streetlight flickered outside, casting a patch of abnormally green light onto the curtain. He got out of bed and went to the window. Beyond the bare rock at the edge of the car park, in the dark blue sky Olly could see strange greenish wisps of cloud shimmering and rippling, as if someone had taken a time-lapse sequence, saturated the colours a bit and then speeded it up. It took him a few minutes before he knew for certain what he was looking at: the northern lights. When the colours started changing from a luminous green to blood red, he quickly got dressed, put on his coat, grabbed the car key and his dad's camera bag, and went outside.

At first, he sat in the passenger seat and watched it all through the dirty windscreen. Then as the lightshow became more vivid, Olly opened the sunroof to rest the camera on the roof of the SUV, because he'd forgotten to bring his dad's tripod. But the action going on in the northern sky was difficult to capture given the glare of the nearby streetlamp and the row of cars in the foreground was spoiling the photos.

Olly looked around, but there was no one else who'd ventured out to see the midnight spectacle. A week before his seventeenth birthday, his dad had taken him to a car park on the industrial estate near their flat, where he was allowed to drive even though he was under-age, because it was not a public highway and therefore didn't count. Surely it wouldn't matter if he drove the car to the top corner of the car park, since this was technically private land too?

Olly eased into the driving seat and adjusted the rearview mirror. He hadn't driven a car since he'd failed his driving test in July. The SUV was much bigger than their Peugeot estate back home, and it felt like he was driving a lorry as he edged slowly out of the parking space and started to drive up to the top of the car park. When he got there, he couldn't find a space big enough to park, but he spotted an exit onto a narrow, unmade road, which Olly assumed was also private. If he drove a little higher up the hill, he would be able to get an even better view. The pitted road surface was full of muddy puddles and the SUV splashed through them in a low gear. Once the road widened a little and levelled out, Olly pulled over, secured the handbrake and stared, dumbfounded. The sky was totally alive now, dancing with colours that seemed to be responding to a strange inaudible rhythm, changing at random intervals as a new burst of energy pulsed through the upper atmosphere.

Olly switched his dad's camera onto manual, gripped it against the neoprene edge of the sunroof and waited patiently for the exact moment when the aurora was at its most spectacular before pressing the shutter. Every time he took what he thought was his best shot, he had a fluttering sensation in his stomach, as though the northern lights were happening inside him. And after each click of the shutter, the aurora, as if keen to impress him even more, went into a new gear, cycling through all its best moves. For a few precious minutes, Olly felt at one with the universe, as if this incredible cosmic display had been put on just for him. Sol would probably have said something profound about human consciousness merging with infinity. Whatever: it was totally epic, but Sol was not here to share it. When the sky quietened down again to inky blackness, Olly wept.

14

Sean woke with an almighty headache that blurred his vision. He picked up his watch and held it close to his face to see what time it was. Gone seven and still dark outside. The single bed next to his was empty; rumpled sheets but no sign of Olly. He pulled on yesterday's clothes, burped and ran a hand through his knotted hair, scanning the rest of the room for clues. He noticed that Olly's parka wasn't strewn across the armchair and the car key was not where he'd tossed it last night.

'What are you up to now, you little beggar…'

He half-strode, half-swayed down to the hotel lobby, expecting to find Olly tucking into a mountain of food in the breakfast room, but he wasn't there.

Outside there was a slash of daylight creeping up from the eastern horizon. Sean walked out of the lobby and round to the back of the hotel where he'd parked the night before, tripping over his undone bootlaces.

Strangely, the SUV was facing in the opposite direction and parked further up the hill than where he remembered leaving it. He definitely hadn't left it with the sunroof wide open. The white sides of the vehicle and the high wheel arches were also totally caked with mud, as if it had been driven off road. Odd, because so far, they'd stuck religiously to Route One. He peered in through the window. The passenger seat was fully reclined, and lying there with his parka draped over him, was Olly, fast asleep, phone in hand.

Sean opened the door and Olly woke with a start, clutching at his coat for protection.

'OK, wakey-wakey, what's the story Mr Midas? If this is some kind of protest because I was snoring, then you're way out of line. I didn't think I needed to say that driving this vehicle is absolutely off limits.'

'You were snoring, but…'

'But what?'

At that moment, Sean caught sight of his camera bag in the footwell beside Olly's feet.

'Jesus, Olly! What the fuck were you thinking taking my camera without asking me?' His voice rose to a peculiar octave. It was obvious he was more angry about Olly taking his camera than driving the hire car. Clearly, in Sean's book, both actions trumped being worried about his child going AWOL.

'Sorry Dad, but you were flat out. You missed it.'

'Missed what?'

'The Northern Lights.'

Olly picked up the camera from the driver's seat beside him, turned it on and flicked through twenty or so stunningly crisp images of rippling pinks, greens, and reds above the dark outline of the mountain behind their hotel. Sean stared in disbelief, swaying slightly.

'It was amazing, Dad. I only took the car a little way up the private road behind the hotel to get a better view. I'm sorry.'

Olly hung his head and waited for his father's vitriolic anger to kick in. But he seemed to be speechless, so Olly handed back the car key, slid his parka on and trudged back to the hotel.

15

'Which Anton? Mum's friend who's into Bitcoin and sports cars?'

'We only know one Anton, Olly, so yes, that guy.'

'He's cool. What's he doing in Iceland?'

'Horse-riding, apparently.'

'For a living?'

'No, don't be dumb: for a holiday. He texted me this morning and said he had something he wanted to tell me in person. It's weird, because I was just thinking about him the day before yesterday. We're going to meet up with him this evening.'

'We are? Where?'

'A horse farm near Djúpivogur. It's not far off piste.'

'Off piste? Is that a drinking metaphor?'

'Off piste, you know, off the beaten track.'

'Can't you just talk in regular English, Dad?'

Olly put on his headphones and for the rest of the journey proceeded to listen to thrash metal at full volume to drown out his father's presence. But the sound couldn't mask the sweaty, boozy smell. Or negate the fact that they were deviating from their planned itinerary by meeting up with Anton. Anton, the crazy guy with a permanent suntan and a gold tooth, who never seemed to have a job but always seemed to have plenty of money. The guy who came over to Kilburn every few months to sit on a kitchen stool and tell Olly's mother wild stories and awful jokes while she cooked dinner. The only guy who could make her laugh until her sides ached, apparently. Anton was funny and relaxed and enthusiastic in a way Olly's dad wasn't. Sean was way too uptight when he was sober or way too incoherent when he was drunk to make Olly's mum laugh like that. Come to think of it, even though alcohol was involved whenever Anton came over, Olly's dad didn't consume any and just went to bed early, mumbling something about how he had work to do or an upset stomach. Anyhow, horse-riding in Iceland was just Anton's style, and Olly pictured him in full riding gear, insisting on going bareback, and expecting the horse to go as fast as his sports car.

The horse farm was owned by an ex-racehorse breeder called Ólafur, who also seemed to be growing weed in a polytunnel behind the farmhouse, Sean was amused to discover. Anton was out on a ride when they arrived, and after being plied with several mugs of strong coffee and a lengthy tour of the owner's thoroughbred wall of fame and silverware collection, Anton finally arrived back.

'Bloody thing was half lame,' he complained to no-one in particular, kicking off his riding boots. 'How are you mate?'

'Not bad, not bad.'

Anton pumped Sean's hand for a good half minute before releasing his grip and suggesting they crack open the bottle of Dom Perignon he'd brought with him from 'the best wine shop in Reykjavík'. Sean considered declining by claiming he was 'on the wagon' but decided against it. He could guarantee that either Olly would let on about his recent heavy drinking or else Anton would rumble him somehow. So, he shrugged and Anton asked Ólafur to bring them some champagne glasses.

'How many, Sir?'

'Three. We'd like to drink a toast to your excellent hospitality,' Anton said, grinning. Ólafur smiled politely and turned to Sean.

'And for your son?'

'A coke. A diet coke.'

'Actually, I'd prefer mineral water, thanks.'

'Mineral water? Whatever next! Well then Olly, let's have a look at you. The absolute spit of your lovely mother! What are you up to these days? Got a girlfriend yet? Off to university?'

Olly could feel himself going bright red. He glanced at his father who was frowning slightly, waiting for him to reply.

'I'm… taking a break.'

'Good, good, excellent idea. A gap year?'

'Erm…'

'Olly's had a few issues over the summer and Tess and I thought it best if Olly… erm…'

'Well, that's grand! Do you both eat steak?' Anton enquired, winking at Sean.

'We do indeed.'

'I'm not hungry,' Olly announced.

'Don't be ridiculous. You're always hungry, kiddo.'

'Not tonight, Dad. I'm really tired. Where are we sleeping exactly? I'd like to go to our room.'

Sean looked flustered for a moment, suddenly aware he hadn't completely thought things through, until Anton stepped in and announced they must take the room opposite his, on the first floor.

'Marvellous view of the mountains,' he assured Olly, putting an arm around his shoulder as he led him upstairs. 'I'll get Ólafur to bring you up a sandwich later, how does that sound? Your Dad and I have some catching up to do.'

'OK.'

The room contained a four-poster bed, a huge television, three packets of biscuits, a bowl of fruit and a sofa with only one arm in front of the window. Olly lay on the bed, ate a banana and an apple and watched an Icelandic reality TV show for a while, then grabbed the spare blanket and a pillow and moved across to the sofa with one arm. He didn't want to end up fighting over the duvet with his drunken father. He did, however, want to clean his teeth, but they'd left their suitcases in the SUV and he wasn't going back downstairs to fetch his and risk more awkward existential questions. He reached into his backpack to check his phone, but the battery was dead and the charger was also in the car. So he just lay there, thinking about sleeping next to Sol on the first night of the festival, waking up in the tent together and brewing tea on the little camping stove, the blue flames licking around the edges of the kettle, and how they'd both jumped when it let out its funny whistle.

16

There was a sandwich on the coffee table beside him when he woke up, the white bread dry and curling, the meat a strange grey colour. His father was lying fully dressed on top of the four-poster bed, looking equally grey. Olly drank some water from the tap in the en-suite bathroom and, feeling peckish, went downstairs. Anton was eating breakfast in the lounge, sporting a white linen napkin under his chin and a black eye.

'Ah, good morning! Come join me, Olly-Moo.'

Olly cringed to hear his childish nickname being used by someone who wasn't even family.

'Did you sleep OK? Your father says you're on tablets to help your, erm… frame of mind.'

'He told you that?'

'Well, let's just say we got a few things out in the open last night. It's what old friends and rivals do. But hey, there's no shame in taking medication. I've been on something for years. Beats feeling like crap every day, that's what I say.'

Olly was not sure whether he wanted to continue with such a personal topic of conversation, but he'd never met an adult who admitted to being on anti-depressants before. At least that's what he thought Anton was getting at.

'Tea or coffee?'

'Orange juice, please.'

Anton poured Olly a large glass.

'Thanks,' he said, managing a smile.

'You look just like your mother aged twenty when you do that,'

Anton remarked cheerfully, the skin around his black eye creasing into purple folds. 'Here, help yourself to toast and jam, Olly,' he said, passing him a clean plate.

'Have you known my mum that long?'

'Yes indeedy. In fact, we were dating each other back then,' he said wistfully, his fingers gently probing the black eye. 'Until she met your father.'

'Really?' Olly said guardedly, not sure if he wanted to hear the lurid details of his parents' origin story from Anton.

'Yes, she was the love of my life, if I'm honest Olly, but it all ended in mayhem and melodrama when your father came along!' Anton closed his eyes and added, 'I hear you're not averse to a bit of drama either...'

Olly stopped buttering his toast and looked up, confused. What exactly had his dad told him?

'It wasn't my fault. It wasn't anyone's fault.'

'Yep. Funnily enough, that's exactly what I told your dad last night. What did you think of the horse meat sandwich I sent up for you, by the way? Delicious, isn't it?'

Olly remembered the leathery grey filling and suddenly lost his appetite. Anton stood up and dusted crumbs from his polo neck with the linen napkin.

'Your dad says you're both here to get a dose of 'big nature', is that right? So how about we take the horses up into the Highlands this morning? Have you ever ridden before?'

'No. Nor has Dad.'

'Oh, I'm not waiting around for your old man. He'll be flat out til lunchtime, the amount he drank last night.'

'Erm…' Olly was struggling to come up with a reason not to go. Part of him wanted to spend longer with Anton, to be sucked into his spontaneous optimism for a few hours and experience the Highlands with him, that vast, crazy-sounding wilderness his dad had mentioned. Because so far everything apart from his private northern lights experience had been a bit tame. In fact, Olly felt like he'd been indoors most of the time they'd been in Iceland: either in the car, in a hotel room, or in a restaurant. What was the point when there was all this incredible stuff to see outdoors? Anton was right: wasn't that what this trip was supposed to be all about?

At that moment Sean walked in, saw his child smiling up at Anton with open admiration, and winced.

'Pack your bag kiddo, we're out of here. I've paid Ólafur for the room.'

'No need to leave yet, pal.' Anton looked mildly offended.

'Olly, get a move on. I've managed to get a dentist appointment in Seyðisfjörður at ten. It's bloody miles away but it was the only place that would see me. If we go now, I'll just about make it in time.'

Without waiting for his son to reply, Sean turned and walked out of the lounge, one hand zipping his coat up, the other cradling his jaw.

17

Olly strapped himself in, put his phone on to charge and stared at the empty battery symbol, his mind at an equally low ebb. His dad drove the SUV out of the farmyard so recklessly they almost collided with Anton's red sports car. A black farm collie was running alongside the vehicle, barking goodbye.

'Bloody animal, get out of the way!'

'Careful Dad, you might run him over.'

Sean scoffed dismissively but slowed down as they approached the gate and waited while Olly got out to open it, drumming his fingers on the steering wheel. Despite having had no coffee since yesterday lunchtime, his heart was racing from all the champagne and painkillers. He was pretty sure he shouldn't be driving, the amount he'd had. But the road was empty and the visibility was good, so he would just have to chance it.

They skirted the headland and turned into a narrow fjord flooded with morning sunlight, the sound of the car's engine sending a flock of white seabirds wheeling into the sky. On the north-facing side, the mountain was coated with patchy snow which the sun hadn't melted all summer long, and, on the opposite bank, even from a distance the mica in the bare granite sparkled. As they rounded the head of the fjord, Sean flipped the sun visor down and clawed around in the seat pocket for his Raybans, cursing as he cut into the gravel on the verge. Olly grabbed the steering wheel to stop the vehicle veering off the road into the fjord.

'Hey, leave the driving to me from now on, kiddo!'

Olly thought about turning on the radio in a bid to discourage his father from speaking, but decided against it. Instead, he went for the direct approach.

'So, what happened between you and Anton last night?'

'Huh?'

'He seemed to have a black eye this morning and from what he said to me at breakfast, you two had a heart-to-heart.'

'Real men don't have heart-to-hearts, Olly.'

'Real men? What's that supposed to mean?'

'Nothing.'

'Well, you must have talked about stuff, because he knows I'm on Prozac. So's he, as a matter of fact.'

'What?'

'Oh, didn't he mention that to you, then?'

'To be honest, I was so angry I can't remember what he said exactly; let's just say it's left a nasty taste in my mouth.'

'That'll be the charcoal toothpaste you use; it's disgusting.'

Sean slowed down to glance at his son and decided it was meant as a joke.

'Very funny, Olly.'

And then, miraculously, they both laughed.

18

Sean lay back and opened his mouth, staring up into the silver-white haze of the dentist's lamp. The brunette dentist with nice calves poked and prodded around his swollen gum and made comments in Icelandic to her assistant, who dutifully wrote everything down. She seemed to be counting his teeth as if they were a flock of sheep and was worried there was one missing. But it was bleeding obvious which one was missing. The question was, why was it hurting so fucking much?

'It's an abscess,' she said finally, rolling back on her chair and pulling the mask away from her mouth. She had beautiful straight white teeth and the curve of her top lip was quite distracting. Sean looked back at the lamp.

'Is it going to hurt like this forever?'

'Only for a couple more days, just until the antibiotics I'm going to give you start to work. Do you have any questions, Sean?'

He bristled at the unexpected use of his first name, the sexily sibilant way she pronounced it, the outrageous informality to be spoken to so intimately by an attractive healthcare professional while still supine.

'No, I don't think so.'

'Well, if you feel unwell over the next few days, give me a ring. Here's my number.' She handed him a business card, and they made eye contact. He tried desperately to read her expression: was this a come-on? Surely there was some kind of unspoken invitation in those pale green eyes? He realised they were almost the same colour as Tess's, and that's what broke the spell.

'One more thing,' she said in a whisper as her assistant left the room,

'I can tell you like it, but alcohol is absolutely forbidden until you finish the course of tablets.'

'Right. Yes, absolutely,' Sean lisped, and realised too late he was mimicking her accented emphasis.

She eyed him coldly for a moment and then turned away to lay out her surgical instruments for the next patient.

19

Seyðisfjörður was a tiny town of colourful houses with white window frames and corrugated metal roofs. Olly paced up and down the various streets and alleyways, encountering the odd cat and breathing in a sour, fishy smell. In the minimart, sheep's faces stared up at him from the chest freezer, and he helped a little girl choose a strawberry lollipop. He bought a lemon one for himself, then, after peeling off the wrapper and popping it into his mouth, he headed over to see if the old wooden church was open.

Religion had played virtually no part in Olly's upbringing, and sometimes he wondered if its absence was adding to his poor mental health. Sol on the other hand was descended from a long line of Polish Jews and went to synagogue every week. They celebrated Passover, Yom Kippur, Rosh Hashanah and Hannukah every year. Olly wasn't sure what they all were, but he liked the way the names sounded and when Sol talked knowledgeably about family customs it made Olly feel like his own family celebrated things without really believing in them. Christmas and Easter were just about buying stuff or eating stuff. It occurred to him that pagan events meant more to his schoolmates than the Christian ones; Hallowe'en for instance was a big deal, but at the same time it felt lame and too American. It was as if no-one gave any thought to what customs stood for anymore. Or even what people themselves stood for.

Olly opened the door to the church and stepped inside. The walls were covered in vertical wood panelling, and the altar at the far end was draped in a white cloth with a single candle burning and a brass cross hanging over it. He slipped into one of the pews, removed the lollipop from his mouth and lay it on the shelf in front of him. He wondered how you get going if you wanted to pray, if there was something you were supposed to do in order to get God's attention. He slid onto his knees, closed his eyes, and put his sticky hands together like a small child. He could hear people arriving in the porch behind him, but he forced them out of his mind. He was trying to drive everything out of his mind. He conjured up an image of the beaker of clear glacier water he'd drunk at the lagoon as if it was a magic potion, the clean white altar cloth hanging in front of him like a sheet and then saw himself walking into it, like he was merging with a blizzard. The voices in the porch were still there, but further away, their rustling coats turning into rustling sheets, until suddenly he sensed Sol was there beside him, singing long, clear notes that floated up into the space above Olly's head and swirled around. His scalp tingled and he wondered what was happening, whether the people behind him could hear Sol too. He felt moved and embarrassed, unable to open his eyes for fear of everyone staring at him and thinking, why was this eighteen-year-old mess from Kilburn kneeling in an Icelandic church all by himself? He heard someone chuckle and when he finally opened his eyes, an old lady who looked like his Scottish Granny was standing in the aisle, clapping her knitted mittens together. At first Olly thought she was applauding him, but then he realised she was just trying to warm herself up.

'It's cold today, isn't it?' she said to him in English. 'Perhaps snow.'

'Perhaps,' Olly replied, as he eased himself back onto the pew and shoved the lemon lollipop into his pocket.

20

After eating some kind of lamb stew in the local cafe, both father and son felt warm and somewhat restored to an easy equilibrium. Sean was browsing leaflets near the entrance and Olly was playing a game on his phone.

'Fancy a little hike, Olly-Moo?'

'Maybe. Where to?'

'This outdoor sculpture thing, dunno what it is but it looks interesting. It was made by a German bloke.' Sean passed him a leaflet with photographs of some concrete domes sticking out of a mountainside.

'OK.'

They returned to the SUV to put on their hiking boots, then set off up the road leading out of town along the edge of the fjord. An enormous ship was gliding up the fjord, its upper desk almost level with the crest of the mountain on the other side.

'Wow, where's that come from?'

'The Faroe Islands, probably. And before that, Denmark.'

'Is it a cruise ship?'

'I think this one's technically a ferry; the Icelanders don't like cruise ships very much.'

'Why's that? Don't they bring tourism?'

'Yes and no: the tourists get off, have a look round, then get back on board the ship again without spending any money, so they don't actually help the local economy.'

They started climbing up the mountainside along a path that cut through grass and gorse and heather, both getting out of breath and stopping every now and then to take in the view and gauge what deck they were now level with on the ship.

'How are you feeling, Olly?' Sean asked as they stopped beside a granite outcrop.

'Unfit.'

'I mean emotionally.'

'I was going to ask you the same thing, Dad.'

'Well then, you go first.'

'I'm missing Mum. And I'm… worried about your drinking. And I'm mad at you for not letting us go horse-riding with Anton this morning. Although I probably would have hated it. And I'm sorry I messed up. This summer, I mean. Is that what you're looking for?'

'Sort of. I miss your Mum too. I'm sorry about spoiling Anton's plans. Actually, sorry-not-sorry, if I'm honest. We had a bit of a disagreement last night. And just so you know, the dentist told me I can't drink while I'm taking her medicine. Is that what you were wanting to hear?'

'Sort of.'

'And… I'd like to be a better parent, Olly. But your mum has set the bar very high.'

'You're doing OK, Dad. And I'd stay away from bars if I were you.'

Sean chuckled.

'You're funny, Mr Midas, did you know that?'

Olly shrugged and flicked his fringe off his face.

'Look, the sculpture thing is just up there!'

Sean followed in his son's footsteps, counting each one to keep his mind off the toothache. He was feeling unusually sweaty and his heart was thumping. Must be the effects of the antibiotics he took at lunchtime.

As he entered the first dome of the artwork, Sean was struck by its strangely urban smell and acoustics. The damp concrete reminded Sean of his first job on a building site after he came down to London to look for work. He'd ended up lugging bags of cement and steel reinforcement bars for a local builder. He pictured how this structure might have looked before they poured the concrete: a skeleton of mild steel rods curving towards the ground, like a giant spider crouching on the mountainside.

Pacing the perimeter of the dome, he heard a long, low mellow note reverberating through the concrete structure. Then the note changed, harmonising with its echo, and there were lyrics he didn't recognise, something about fire and ice, about continents breaking apart. He was so taken aback by the purity of the voice and the sincerity of the words, it took Sean a minute or two to realise it was his own son singing. He wanted to call out and say how lovely it sounded, but he didn't want Olly to stop. He had never heard him sing before, never even knew he had such a beautiful voice.

In the adjacent dome, Olly sat cross-legged facing out through the arched entrance, a tear trickling down his face as he finally let go, releasing everything he'd been bottling up inside into waves of sound encased in clouds of steam as he sang into the cold air. He was trying to remember the words he and Sol had scribbled on the back of a toilet cubicle door in a Sharpie pen after they got high that night. He remembered Sol showing him how to use his falsetto voice to sing the high part. And the feeling of the two of them merging together as the intervals between their voices got closer, until they were singing in delicious unison.

Olly stopped singing and a solitary echo slowly faded away through the concrete chamber. He pulled out his phone, because he felt that now would be the perfect moment for Sol to send him a text. But there was no message. Olly took a selfie instead, thought about texting it to Sol, and then deleted it. He must have sent at least twenty texts by now, but he still had no idea whether the phone was even in Sol's possession. For all he knew, it might still be in that ziplock bag in a filing cabinet at the police station. What was Sol thinking right now? Was it over between them? How long do you wait? Olly had no idea what happens after you realise you love someone but before you've plucked up the courage to tell them.

He got up off the floor and wandered back into the other chamber to find his dad playing air guitar. Olly joined in for a moment.

'Amp not working?'

'No, it's on full, but only in my head.'

'You should play for real, Dad.'

'Are you kidding, I wouldn't know where to start.'

'I can show you the basics, if you like. When we get back to London.'

Sean's hands dropped back by his sides.

'I was going to teach you the basics of photography on this trip, but you seem to have figured it out just fine by yourself, judging by those photos you took the other night. You've got a real knack for it, Olly.'

'A friend taught me. They have a similar camera to yours.'

'Well, at least now I can boast that you inherited some of your DNA from me.'

'Yeah, it was winding me up every time Anton said I looked like Mum.'

'You have no idea how much that wound me up too, kiddo.'

'Dad, would you mind not calling me *kiddo* anymore? I really hate it.'

'Sure. Sorry.'

21

'Mum?'

'Hi darling, where are you now?'

'A hotel in a place called Egilsstaðir. Are you in the New Forest?'

'We're leaving in about an hour. I managed to find everything except the camping kettle. Do you have any idea where it is?'

Olly realised it was one of the things they'd left behind in the aftermath.

'Erm... I'm sorry Mum, it's probably at Jonah's.'

'Jonah?'

'You know, the guy whose Mum gave us a lift to the festival.'

'Oh. Never mind, I'm sure Eddie will bring one.'

'Who's Eddie?'

'Just someone from work, you don't know her.'

'Oh, I thought Eddie was a man.'

'Don't be silly darling, why would I go camping with another man?'

There was a weird pause. Olly wondered whether he should mention that they'd seen Anton.

'Anyway, what have you been up to today?'

'Me and Dad hiked halfway up a mountain.'

'You didn't make it to the top?'

'No, but we climbed up as far as this cool sculpture by a German artist.'

'Ah, I'm glad your dad is managing to fit in a few cultural things too, that's nice. Good for your general education. You know, good for your UCAS form.'

'Mum I'm not here so I've got extra things to put in my personal statement for uni.'

'I know, I know, I'm just saying that sounds fun, that's all.'

'Can you put your camera on?'

Olly flipped over onto his stomach and bunched up the pillows so he could prop his phone against the headboard. When she appeared on his screen, his mother looked different somehow. Her face was puffier than usual and there were sad creases around the edges of her eyes.

'Are you OK, Mum?'

'Yes, why do you ask?'

'It feels like you and Dad aren't getting on. Is it to do with Anton?'

'Anton?' His mother's green eyes opened wide.

'Yeah. We met up with him yesterday.'

'What? How come?' his mother stammered. Then her mood changed, and she said airily, 'Come to think of it, Anton was talking about going horse-riding in Iceland last time he came over.'

Olly could hear his father's footsteps outside in the corridor. Now was not the right time to ask her about Anton, and anyway it was none of his business.

'Dad's back now Mum, gotta go. Love you.'

He hung up and tidied his things off the bedside table to make space for their room picnic and went to fetch the toothbrush glasses from the bathroom for their bottled water. His dad's glass was already rimmed with charcoal scum from his toothpaste and his packet of antibiotics was standing beside it. The label said, printed in English, 'DO NOT DRINK ALCOHOL WHILE TAKING THIS MEDICATION'.

But that didn't stop Sean from arriving back with two cans of beer.

'Who are those for?' Olly asked as soon as he set them down on the table.

'I thought we could have one each. It's the low alcohol type.'

'Nice try, Dad.' Olly swiped them both out of his father's hand and lobbed them into the wastepaper bin. Sean frowned, took a deep breath and then puffed out his cheeks. Olly took the shopping bag, placed it on the table and peered inside it.

'Did you get me a salad like I asked?'

'Sorry, they only had hot dogs. And I forgot the mustard.'

22

It had been a long, barren, three-hour drive, first north and then west, to get to Lake Mývatn, where Sean was supposed to be following up on a photo shoot of a geothermal plant he did for National Geographic during his last visit to Iceland five years ago. His jaw was feeling less sore, but his nerves were frayed and all the medication was giving him stomach-ache. Or perhaps he was still feeling out of sorts about his conversation with Anton the other evening. At any rate, things seemed to have improved somewhat between him and Olly, which he had wanted to report to Tess last night, only she wasn't picking up.

There had been a slight fracas this morning when they'd driven ten miles out of Egilsstaðir before Sean realised they were low on petrol and had to turn back. He bought Olly a bag of doughnuts by way of an apology, but his son turned them down and started eating a banana instead.

'You look different today, Mr Midas, how come?'

'Deal's a deal.'

'What do you mean?'

'Well, since you're not drinking, I cut my fringe.'

'I see. What with?'

'Mum's nail scissors.'

'Bet she'll be mad when she finds out you brought them with you.'

'Nah. She's too shaken up about us running into Anton.'

'Shit Olly, what did you tell her?'

'Not much.'

Olly folded the banana skin in half and lay it in the little trash can between their seats.

'I hope you didn't mention the black eye.'

Olly shot his dad a sideways glance then looked straight ahead.

'Is it off limits to ask about that? Did you guys get into some kind of punch-up?'

'You could say. Anton had it coming. He's been playing with fire for years.'

Olly stared out across the empty mountain pass and wondered what his father meant by this statement. Surely it was not literal? Nevertheless, Olly kept picturing Anton in his riding boots leaping through flames, a glass of champagne in his hand.

They rounded a sharp bend and an impossibly blue lake emitting several plumes of steam came into view.

'Did you just fart, Dad?'

'Haha, just you wait. This is the stinkiest place in Iceland.'

That's a new one, Olly thought: the stinkiest. His dad pulled off Route One into a car park. When they opened the car doors, the sulphurous air was a lot more pungent than either of them was expecting. Olly held his nose and leaned against the side of the SUV while his dad retrieved his camera bag and tripod from the back.

'OK, let's get to work. Sooner I get done here, the sooner we can be wallowing in the Nature Baths.'

23

Wading out to where he could see Olly's dark hair and pale, rounded shoulders from behind, Sean wondered for a moment if he'd mistaken his son for somebody else, because he seemed to be talking to a family who were hanging out in same pool. Even as he got closer, he doubted himself because although it sounded like Olly's voice, he was speaking a different language. It wasn't Icelandic; Sean thought it sounded more slavic, possibly eastern European.

'Rodzina mojego przyjaciela jest polska,' Olly enunciated slowly, tapping his bare chest. The family were nodding and smiling and he was pleased they'd understood. Then, seeing his father approaching, he gave them a little wave and moved off to join him in the next pool over. Olly sank down into the warm, milky water next to Sean, humming under his breath.

'Who were those people you were talking to?'

'They work at the geothermal plant where we just were.'

'What nationality are they?'

'Polish. They told me there are twenty thousand Poles living in Iceland these days.'

'I see. They told you all that in Polish?'

'Yup. Well, with the help of a bit of sign language.'

'Mum didn't tell me you were taking Polish at school.'

'I'm not.'

'But you seemed to know how to say more than a few words of Polish just then.'

Had he not cut his fringe, at this point Olly would have tilted his head to conceal his facial expression, but today he was more exposed.

'My friend taught me.'

'I'm assuming you mean that friend?'

'Huh?'

'The one who spray-painted your coat?'

'Yeah, that friend, Dad.'

In spite of his desire to find out more about Olly's private life, Sean decided not to press any further, for fear of damaging the fragile amnesty they'd only just achieved. He stood up and turned to retrieve his towel from the side of the pool.

Olly felt embarrassed that his father was stark naked in what seemed to him like a public outdoor swimming pool. Then he noticed that on his dad's right butt cheek was a small tattoo. Two words written in curling capitals in a language he didn't recognise: MET TE.

'When did you get that?'

'What?'

'The tat.'

Sean peered round at himself as if he'd totally forgotten he once got inked.

'Oh that. Let's just call it one of life's many mistakes. No, that's not quite true. Mette was not a mistake; but the tattoo was.'

'Who was Mette?'

'My first love, if you really want to know.'

Now it was Olly's turn to contain his surprise and curiosity at this new revelation. He sank down lower in the water until the surface was level with his nostrils like a hippo, waiting to see if his father was going to add any more details.

Sean spread his arms along the edge of the pool, trying to get comfortable with the idea of having a man-to-man conversation with his teenage son. He closed his eyes, remembering the little tattoo parlour they'd gone to in Ísafjörður, where Mette sat on a stool next to him, holding his hand while the artist worked away, stabbing his rear end with a needle.

'I was mad about her, Olly. She was the most beautiful girl I'd ever met. Until I met your mother, of course. It was my first time in Iceland. I came with a mate who was studying photography like me. We planned to hitchhike round the country and shoot a load of different places together, but I dropped my bloody camera on the second day and then, as I was drowning my sorrows in a bar downtown, this tall, gorgeous girl came up and asked me how I could look so miserable in such a beautiful country. We got talking, and you know – or maybe you don't – we just clicked. I spent the next two weeks in her pocket, so to speak, and when it came to our last day, I wanted something to remember her by. She was going back to Denmark. It hurt like hell, actually.'

'Parting from her or getting the tattoo?'

'Well, both, if I'm honest.'

'Figures.'

Olly's face wore that same intense expression that Sean remembered seeing when Olly was a little kid listening to one of his lurid adventures after he came back from a trip abroad. It made Sean suddenly want to hug him. Instead, a long but comfortably manly silence passed between them.

Then Olly asked, 'What does Mum think about your tattoo?'

'What do you think?'

Olly made a cartoonish gesture of swiping a blade across his neck.

'You got it.' Sean rolled his eyes and arched his back, stretching out sideways before sinking down into the water.

'Were you in love?'

'With your mum?'

'No, with Mette.'

'Probably.'

'How did you know?'

'The usual physiological clues.'

'I don't mean were you physically attracted, I mean, did you *love* her?'

'At that age I didn't know there was a difference.'

'Well, there is.'

Sean looked sideways at his son. He didn't know what to make of the defiant edge in Olly's voice, but he suspected it meant he was missing something important, something that would be patently obvious to Tess.

24

'Jesus Dad, why do you have to keep messing up our itinerary like this? I can't stand it when you change the plan without telling me. Húsavík's another forty miles out of our way! I thought you said you've got work to do and deadlines to meet? Who is this person we need to visit?' Olly demanded to know, staring helplessly at the map on his iPhone.

'My former boss at National Geographic. I worked for her back in the good old days. She's retired now. Haven't seen her in years, not since she moved back to Iceland. It would be rude to drive all the way round Iceland and not go and see her.'

'What's her name?'

'Sigríður. But everyone calls her Sigga. You'll love her.'

Olly thought that turning up on your ex-boss's doorstep unannounced was a really bad idea, but he didn't say as much. He began mentally preparing himself for a pointless side trip to see a boring old woman who lived in a remote fishing town.

Things started improving when they pulled up outside the house in Húsavík and an adorable shaggy dog bundled out to meet them, followed by a little boy about six years old wearing purple dungarees. Olly had barely got out of the SUV before the dog was clambering all over him.

'What's his name?' Olly asked the boy, pointing to the dog.

'Apollo,' the boy said shyly.

'Sean Mackie! Is it really you? Come on in! This can't be little Olly, surely?'

Sigríður stood in the doorway with her hands on her hips, wearing a flowery apron and fluorescent orange crocs, her wispy grey-brown hair blowing about in the breeze. The child slipped his hand into his grandmother's and led her back indoors. Olly and Sean followed, the dog bringing up the rear.

The house was pleasantly cosy and bohemian to Olly's eyes, every corner and every surface filled with ethnic rugs and paintings, curios and keepsakes. There was a large table in the middle of the kitchen where Sigga and the child – who turned out to be called Roman – were playing with salt dough.

'Would you like some coffee, Sean? Will you be staying for lunch? Need a bed for the night?'

'Coffee would be great, thanks Sigga, but we're booked into a place in Akureyri this evening.'

'I'll brew it nice and strong, just how you like it. Now tell me all your news, how's Tess doing? Did she launch her business – when was it I last saw you? Must be seven or eight years ago, certainly before little Roman was born.'

'Tess is doing fine, thanks, she's very busy, but the business seems to be finally taking off, yes.'

'And Olly, I don't believe we've ever actually met, but your dad has shown me pictures of you and of course I always loved getting your mother's homemade family Christmas card every year and seeing how much you'd grown.'

Olly flashed her a quick smile and carried on coiling a salt dough sausage into a miniature beehive. Fascinated, Roman watched him for a while and then ran off to get something. Sigga poured the coffee and continued, undeterred by Olly's reluctance to speak.

'You like making things, Olly? I bet you're super creative, like your Mum and Dad.'

'He took some great photos of the aurora the other night, didn't you Olly?'

Olly coloured up; even though he was pleased that his dad thought enough of the photos to mention them to his old boss.

'And he's got a great singing voice. Shame none of us get to hear it.'

Olly went redder still.

'Well, you're in the right place; everyone loves singing in Iceland! You should join a choir, Olly. Do they have one at your school?'

'No,' he lied. 'But I'm thinking of starting a band.'

This piece of information stood stark naked in their midst as Olly tried to figure out why he'd said it. He'd barely even thought about it as an idea. Perhaps he'd crumbled under the social pressure of the situation or given in to his usual desire to please. Did he really want to be in a band? His Mum would never let him, that's for sure. She'd have a million reasons why it was a terrible idea, starting with the obvious: sex, drugs and alcohol.

He felt someone tugging the bottom of his sweatshirt and turned round to see Roman looking up at him, holding out a gluestick and a pot of pink glitter. Olly smiled and started rolling out another piece of salt dough and handing Roman a heart-shaped cookie cutter. The child pressed out three hearts, pointing at himself, his grandmother and Olly, to let him know who they were for.

'You've scored a hit with our little Roman,' Sigga said, laughing as she piled her wayward hair up into a bun.

The little boy opened the gluestick and daubed the three hearts before sprinkling glitter onto each one. Olly caught his father's eye and knew exactly what he was thinking as Roman lifted up the hearts and shook them one by one, watching the fine flakes of pink glitter falling like snow onto the kitchen table. Picking up a cocktail stick, Roman stabbed each heart in turn, wiggling the stick around to make sure it made a nice, round hole.

'Allt búið!' Roman said, clapping his hands together, glitter flying everywhere.

'All done!' Sigga interpreted, laughing. 'Shall we thread ribbons through your necklaces? I think I've got some in my needlework basket.' She walked off into the sitting room to look for it.

Sean sipped his coffee and gazed out at the back garden where Sigga had hung up a bird feeder. Blue tits and sparrows were taking turns to feed on the nuts, cheeping happily and flitting from branch to branch outside the window. He felt a sense of calm being here and realised that for as long as he'd known her, Sigga's warm, maternal energy had guided him in his adult life in a way his own mother never had. Like the time when he and Tess almost split up, Sigga had changed her work schedule so she could meet him in London and give him advice and emotional support, and when Olly was born, Sigga was one of the first people to pay them a visit in Kilburn. In fact, his mother, who'd only just arrived herself, had been most put out when Sean had reacted more enthusiastically to seeing Sigga on his doorstep than the reception he'd given her. But then, unlike his mother, Sigga

listened and was patient. She expected effort and results, and when
you brought good work to show her, she rewarded you with praise
and encouragement. Maybe that's what he needed to do more often
with Olly. Maybe he should try using Sigga as his role model when it
came to parenting.

The dog must have heard something and started rushing around
the kitchen, barking to be let out into the hallway. Olly opened the
door to the hallway and Apollo skidded out onto the wooden floor,
leaving a trail of pink glittery paw-prints. Sean smiled as he opened his
pot of antibiotics, tipped a tablet into his palm and washed it down
with the dregs of his coffee.

'Glitter everywhere! Tess would be having kittens,' Sean chuckled
to himself as he rinsed his empty mug under the tap.

25

'Jeez Dad, that's another forty miles out of our way.'

'Gimme a break, Olly; it was an accident, I didn't forget them on purpose. And at least Sigga found my tablets and rang me before we got all the way to Akureyri.'

'I didn't forget mine on purpose, Dad, if that's what you're implying. Just saying.'

Sean swung into the next lay-by beside a wide, braided riverbed to turn the SUV around and head back to Húsavík.

Olly looked down the long, straight road that ran north alongside a river and sighed, knowing they were about to traverse it for the second time that day. He glanced back over his shoulder, in the direction they should have been going, and it was only then that he noticed a snow-capped mountain range off to the left, glistening in the far distance against an angry, grey sky.

'What's that over there?' he asked his father.

'It's the Highlands, remember? I told you about them. Iceland's answer to Mordor. NASA trained their astronauts for the Apollo missions there, before they went to the moon.'

'Seriously? Trained them to do what?'

'To do rock sampling. The middle of Iceland is not just an arctic wilderness, it's also a geological wonderland. Only in the summer months, mind you. In winter it's treacherous and the rivers are too deep to drive through.'

'Aren't there any bridges?'

'Hardly.'

'Have you ever been?'

'No,' his father replied wistfully.

'Is that why you rented this kind of vehicle?'

'Not at all, I just wanted something rugged and safe for our trip.'

As if to demonstrate this point, Sean put his foot on the accelerator and they sped back down the road they'd just driven. Olly found himself gazing out across the desolate terrain beside the road, toying with mental images of men in white spacesuits, bouncing in slow motion off the windy tundra.

26

'Back so soon?' Sigga joked. 'Actually it's a good job, because I made too much fish soup.'

Apollo bustled round them, sniffing and greeting them like old friends.

'Where's Roman?' Olly asked as they took their boots off.

'Well, your Dad's not the only one around here who needs to remember his medicine. Roman does too. He's quite poorly, actually, although he doesn't look it. He has chronic kidney disease. That's why he lives with me here and not with his mother in America. He needs to have dialysis every day and it's very expensive over in the States. He's upstairs now, sleeping.'

After Olly went to wash his hands upstairs, he peeked round the door into Roman's room. He knew which one it was because the door handle was covered in pink glitter. The child was lying on his back with his arms by his head, fast asleep in his purple dungarees while a machine beside him whirred away doing its job. It looked like Olly's mum's new printer, only it had red tubes coming out of it that went into Roman's thin little arm.

Olly picked up the stuffed T-Rex sprawled across the armchair in the corner and sat down. All the storybooks on the shelf to his right were in Icelandic, apart from a hardback called 'Now We Are Six'. He pulled it down and opened the front cover. Inside, someone had written a message:

Happy Birthday Roman, I hope you'll be six now 'for ever and ever',
love from Uncle Magnus

Olly slid it back where he found it, wondering what kind of person Roman's Uncle Magnus was.

There was a row of plastic action figures on the windowsill, all facing into the street, as if longing to be allowed out on an adventure. Some were posing impatiently, hands on hips, a soldier in a green uniform was missing an arm, one guy was carrying a large hammer. And at the end of the row Olly noticed a spaceman in a white suit with massive boots. He walked over and picked it up, peering at the face through the transparent dome of his helmet until he realised you could press a button on the side of its head and make the visor flip open.

The tiny click it made was enough to wake Roman, who looked scared when he saw someone standing at the end of his bed.

'Hey,' Olly said softly, 'It's only me.'

The boy looked at him with wide grey eyes, as if he barely remembered they'd played together earlier that morning. Then he sat up and held his arms out. Olly wasn't sure what he was supposed to do; the machine was still working and attached to Roman, so he couldn't exactly lift him up. Instead, he knelt down next to the bed. Roman put his arms around his neck and they hugged each other for what felt like forever. Olly could sense that familiar tidal wave of sadness and loneliness brimming up behind his eyes as Roman squeezed him tighter still. He sniffed and the little boy let go, a look of concern and puzzlement on his pale face as he realised Olly was crying.

Roman pointed to a hook on the wall above his bed, where Sigga had hung the three salt-dough hearts, and indicated to Olly that he should take one of them. Olly lifted two down, and put one around the boy's neck, shaking the child's hand like he was awarding him a medal. Then Roman did the same for him, but instead of shaking Olly's hand, he reached up and planted a kiss on the top of his head.

When they finally cruised into Akureyri which – as Sean couldn't resist informing Olly was Iceland's second biggest settlement – it was already dark. The forecast was for snow, and the snowflake symbol on the dashboard indicated it was freezing outside. Sean was feeling twitchy; it was coming up to 4pm when the Vínbúðin would be closing. He had to remind himself that he was off the booze, which made a wave of irritation rear up inside him, causing him to speed through a red light.

'Jesus! Steady on, Dad. No need to test the airbags. It's the next turning on the right,' Olly said, grabbing onto the dashboard.

Most of the hotels in town were fully booked that night and Sean hadn't been able to get a twin-bedded room. So, he'd rented an apartment with separate bedrooms, which Olly seemed pleased about. And – they discovered when they got there – separate bathrooms. Sean kicked off his boots in the hallway, handed his son a five thousand króna note, and announced he was free to do what he liked that evening.

'So, like, we're not going to get dinner or anything?'

'You can. I'm not really hungry after two bowls of Sigga's fish soup.'

'OK.'

Sean picked up his camera bag, shoved his suitcase along the corridor into the room with the double bed and closed the door. He was in a strange, unsettled mood and he desperately needed to call Tess and find out what exactly was going on. She still hadn't replied to his voice message from last night and now she'd posted something cryptic on Instagram with pictures of her all dressed up on what appeared to be a girls' night out. In all of them, she was posing with what Sean would call her 'flirty face'. Since the pictures were clearly not intended for him, it had made him feel absurdly jealous, and if Anton had not still been out horse-riding somewhere in south Iceland, he would most likely have given him another black eye.

He strode into the en-suite bathroom and peered in the mirror at the infected gap in his gum. Several days' worth of stubble and a failure to pack either a hairbrush or comb for this trip meant he was looking quite dishevelled. Also, there were bags under his eyes, which stared back at him with a mean, piercing look. Who could blame her, he told himself; Tess is no longer married to a stud. Feeling sorry for himself, Sean decided to run a nice hot bath, take his next round of drugs, watch something dark and dirty and then get an early night.

Meanwhile, Olly sat in the other bedroom, still wearing his parka, on the edge of his single bed, plucking up the courage to go off by himself round a strange town in a foreign country. If Sol was there, they would probably be going to some obscure little gig this evening. And afterwards, they'd sneak back into this room and cuddle up in this bed together. He ran the little fantasy sequence a few times, adding extra details, but all manner of complications started occurring to him, as his inner critic asserted itself and tried to derail his imaginary night out. Olly pulled his phone from his backpack and scrolled through all the photos he had of Sol, right back to when they'd first met at Jonah's house party.

He flicked back the other way, looking at the more recent shots he'd taken on his phone in Iceland, and paused when he got to the one he'd taken a week ago of the poster in the guitar shop window in Reykjavík. He zoomed in to check the date and saw that the open mic night was taking place that very evening. Too bad he was going to miss it. But something made him google the location, and he was surprised to discover that The Midas Rooms were actually in Akureyri not Reykjavík, and when he checked the time, Olly realised the event was taking place just down the road in under an hour.

Olly's heart was thudding as he put on his headphones to re-listen to the rough recording he and Sol had made of their song. Was it good enough to perform? Could he remember the chords? Could he sing it by himself without Sol's harmony part? Could he even find the courage to get up on stage? Through the fabric of his T-shirt, he felt Roman's salt-dough heart hanging round his neck and decided he had nothing to lose.

Stuffing the króna in his pocket, he changed into his other sweatshirt (the hoodie that Sol called his 'cool one'), put his parka and backpack back on, and went out, slamming the front door of their apartment before he realised he'd left his phone on the bed. He also hadn't remembered to take a key with him. Never mind, his dad would no doubt still be up when he got back.

28

There was a brisk, arctic wind in his face as he walked due north along the street towards the centre of town. Since they were almost at 66 degrees north and not far from the Arctic Circle, so his dad kept reminding him, Olly imagined this wind commencing at the pole and whistling over thousands of floating icebergs to reach him. Putting his hood up to protect his face from the icy blasts, he peered in the shop windows he passed. Some were full of toy puffins or hand-knitted woollen sweaters, in others there were people drinking beer and eating hamburgers.

He stopped when he came to a golden sign projecting sideways above an entrance a few streets from their apartment. Embossed in a viking-style script were the words 'The Midas Rooms'. Olly sidled up, tingling and wary. The guy on the door charged him 1000 króna to get in and then opened the door for Olly to step inside.

There was a small stage at the far end lit by red, green and blue LED lights, and a handful of people sitting at round tables. Olly couldn't tell who he needed to speak to, so he edged his way past the bar to go to the toilet, hoping that by the time he returned, it would be clear who was in charge of the open mic list. If that was how it worked; he had no idea. Standing in front of the urinals, he panicked: maybe the list was all decided in advance by email, and he wouldn't be able to do his song. The timid part of him decided that this was probably for the best, because he was too nervous anyway. Someone pushed past him and muttered something in Icelandic. He walked back out, went up to the bar and asked the guy who was serving for a glass of water.

'Ice?'

'Sure,' Olly replied, remembering the thousand year old glacier water he'd drunk.

'Something to eat?' He handed Olly a menu.

'No, but…'

'Yes?'

'Who's organising the open mic, I mean who do I ask if I want to, you know… sign up?'

'Tell Þórhildur, she's over by the stage there. In the green sweater.'

Olly glanced across the room and saw a young woman talking to a skinny guy in a beanie hat who was setting up the drum kit. He put his glass of water on an empty table, hung his backpack on the chair, and went across to speak to her, his palms sweating.

'Thor-Hilda?' he asked in a very English accent.

She turned to face him.

'Hæ! Cool coat. Wanna sing something tonight?' she asked.

'Erm, yeah. If there's an electric guitar I could borrow.'

'Sure; we've brought a guitar with us. What's your name?'

'Ol Mackie.'

'Al McKee?'

'Something like that.'

'What's the song?'

'I… I'm gonna sing 'True North'. It's an original.'

'Great, I'll stick you down. It'll be about 9-ish. Is that OK?'

Olly nodded, wiping his palms on the sides of his parka. No turning back now. Returning to his table, he found a crumpled scrap of paper in his backpack and wrote out the lyrics.

The evening started with a comedy act that Olly couldn't understand a word of, and which was only mildly funny, judging by how few people laughed. Then there was a girl who played the harp and sang in a sickly-sweet voice. A group of boys who looked not much older than Olly performed a skit involving a nerf gun and some fake red blood that went everywhere. Þórhildur didn't look too happy about that, because some landed on the cymbals and the drummer was clearly a friend of hers. Then, just as they were trying to clean it up with some paper napkins, Olly heard his name being called. The drummer handed him a battered old acoustic guitar with a very high action. Olly strummed his thumb lightly across the strings and realised he was going to have to quickly tune it. He'd left the lyrics on the table and dithered about whether he should go back and get them. Perhaps he could manage without. Þórhildur patted him on the back and told him to relax and that the floor was his. Whatever that meant.

The stage was still slippery from the red paint and the red lights made it look worse than it already was. He looped the guitar strap over his head, took a deep breath and stepped up to the microphone.

'Hi. My name's Ol. I'm from London. I'm doing a song I wrote this summer. Erm, it's kinda personal. And, er, yeah, I'd like to dedicate it to all of you out there who sometimes feel that the world is a pretty, you know, shitty place.'

'Yeah, man!' someone shouted from the back.

Olly bent over the instrument and tuned it as best he could by ear. Shaking, he tapped the mic and it gave out a crisp, expectant cough. Someone turned all the stage lights blue, and he stared into the centre of the middle one, trying to forget there was an audience sitting right in front of him. The blue light reminded him of the icebergs floating on the glacial lagoon, of the meltwater he'd drunk, and the silent prayer he'd said to whoever. And with that in mind, he began, a little shakily at first, naked without his pedals to distort the sound of the chords, but as he pictured what Sol had written on the back of the toilet cubicle door, he found a deep seam of courage and his voice gained a raw certainty he'd never felt before.

Darkness flows in silent hollows
Encircling my fear
But the needle points true north
When you're near

Love grows in secret kisses
Sealed in with sleep
And the needle points true north
When you're in deep

I lost my compass long ago
And now I'm cast adrift
Watching from the shallows
Hoping change is swift

Slow-moving continents
Our flesh is torn apart
But the needle points true north
With you in my heart

Olly was about to repeat the last two lines of the chorus a few times to finish, but in that moment a final verse came to him, so he sang that instead:

You told me once, I love you
As I stared into your eyes
The needle points true north
Cos the truth never lies

Yeah, the truth never lies

Olly's voice wavered slightly on the final note, a high, heartfelt falsetto, and he felt like that six-year-old version of himself who'd thrown up at the local pool after being made to swim unaided. He strummed one last melancholic chord and let it ring out. For a brief moment he thought he saw Sol's face at the back, watching him. It wasn't of course, but at least they were clapping, and after that everyone joined in. He knew his face was red but no one could tell with the blue light shining on it, so he bowed his head slightly and handed the guitar back to the drummer, who patted him on the back.

'Cool song, Ol, keep practising.'

Olly fumbled his way back to his table, back into the shadows, and promptly knocked over his glass of water. When the glass smashed onto the floor everyone in the bar fell silent. Embarrassed for him, Þórhildur went to get some paper towels from behind the bar and started mopping it up.

'You were great, well done!' she assured him, 'I love your voice; it sounds so vulnerable.'

Olly looked at the two spilled ice cubes standing in a puddle on the table and didn't know what to say.

'Oh no, your coat got wet too.'

When he took off his parka, he saw that Sol's red target was not only wet but had been spattered with some of the fake blood.

'Listen Ol, the last guy on my list hasn't shown up, so we're going to get something to eat now, do you wanna come?' she asked.

Olly wondered if he had enough króna for food. Perhaps he should just go back to the Airbnb, but adrenaline was pumping through his system, nudging him to take a chance.

'Yeah, sure.'

29

After he heard Olly slam the front door, Sean lay on his bed staring at the ceiling. Outside the evening traffic rumbled past his gaping window, headlights swiping across his face as they turned the corner. He was vaguely irritated by it and thought about getting up to close the curtains, but in the absence of alcohol, he also found the sweeping rhythmic beams of light strangely soothing. He was trying to decide what to say to Tess when he spoke to her, trying to work out what he felt about everything, trying to decide who was to blame, who had the right to be angry. Perhaps he shouldn't call her at all and let her get the message that he was angry that way. Why did everything have to be so damn complicated? They'd been married twenty years, dated for at least another two before that, surely almost quarter of a century is enough time for two reasonably intelligent people to have things figured out. But lately, their relationship felt sort of shapeless and indistinct, as if someone had left fingerprints on the camera lens, making all the images fogged and useless.

At this point, he could only be sure of two things: that he loved her, and that he didn't want to lose her. But it felt like she was in the process of losing him, pulling silently away, whether deliberately or not, she'd allowed a gap to open up between them. No, not a gap – a gulf, a chasm – that he somehow couldn't bridge and couldn't remember how it had started. Just like he couldn't remember how his toothache had started: one minute he was fine, and his incisor was intact, and the next his tooth was gone and his jaw hurt like hell.

He put his finger in his mouth and ran it along the side of the offending gum, where the swelling had subsided somewhat. He was pleased that at least his dental problems appeared to be abating; no need to keep popping painkillers every four hours. He could tell Tess that: maybe she'd be pleased that he'd taken appropriate action and found himself a dentist. She was always talking about the importance of self-care. Or maybe she no longer cared about his wellbeing.

With that thought, he shot up from the bed, propelled by his own self-pity, and began pacing up and down the narrow gap beside the bed. The white sheepskin rug started bunching up under his feet and almost tripped him up. He lunged at it, as if it was still animate, kicking it to the other side of the room, where it slumped down by the door, the lamb slain and submissive.

Another wave of anger came over him. He blamed Olly for all of this. It was Olly who had caused the breach between himself and Tess. And then it occurred to him that this was a familiar pattern, that he had always blamed Olly when they'd hit a rough patch. But wasn't Olly the innocent party? Olly was not the one who had made Tess laugh in their Kilburn kitchen on so many occasions that she had succumbed to his charms. Olly was not the one who had turned a blind eye when Tess enthused about Anton a little too often. And as far as Sean knew, Olly had not encouraged his mother to take up with her ex again. How could he have done, when Olly never even knew until this trip that Tess and Anton had once been an item?

Sean dropped to his knees and reached for the sheepskin, cradling it tenderly in his arms, and emitted a strange hiccupping sob. He had a strong urge to apologise to his son, but he didn't know what for. He thought back to the night he'd driven out of London to a police station in the home counties, under strict instructions from Tess to rescue their son from the 'jaws of evil'. Just like she'd characterised this trip to Iceland as saving Olly from harm, saving him from his tendency to be 'his own worst enemy'. Corroborating her take on the situation, the police had told Sean over the phone that Olly was 'distraught, incoherent and inconsolable'. Those were their precise words. And yet, when Sean arrived, his son was sitting meekly on a plastic chair in the corridor, clutching his parka and his phone. When his eyes met Sean's, they were tragically apologetic, so there had been no need to talk on the drive back to London.

Sean sobbed even harder when he realised he'd passed up yet another opportunity that night to connect with Olly, to understand his inner world. Why had he allowed the whole journey to pass in silence? Was this journey around Iceland really an act of penance for Sean, not Olly, so that he could make up for countless previous failures to communicate with his child? What had Olly needed from him that night that he hadn't been able to provide? A shoulder to cry on had always been Tess's department; she was the one their child would instinctively turn to, not Sean.

His emotions switched gears again, as a jealous surge pumped round his body. He realised this familiar discomfort about their mother-son closeness was tinged with a sense of betrayal, of desertion. And with that thought, Sean came full circle: Olly was the reason Tess was distant, because Olly was the one person she could turn to when she needed comfort or companionship, not Sean. Olly was her shoulder to cry on.

Even though Sean knew that this was only a story his ego was making up on the spot in an effort to get the upper hand – or failing that, to get his mood to rally – and even though this was a perfect example of his tendency to indulge in myths and half-truths, he grabbed hold of it, like a rubber ring tossed towards him as he floundered in the open ocean. The rubber ring he should have given to little Olly in the swimming pool years ago, instead of berating him for not trying hard enough. The rubber ring Olly must have needed that night at the police station. Why else would he have disappeared into his room for two weeks after that, failing to show up at mealtimes and, as far as Sean and Tess could work out, not eating, dressing or showering for over a fortnight. Why else would the GP have put him on high-dose anti-depressants after spending the sum total of five minutes talking to Olly alone in his consulting room, while Tess and Sean sat anxiously in the waiting area outside?

Sean sighed, wiped his face on his shirtsleeve and smoothed his hair. He heaved himself back onto his feet and scanned the room for his phone. Needing a change of scene and knowing that these kind of conversations with Tess always went better when he was outside walking, he grabbed his coat and left the apartment to pace the streets of Akureyri.

30

The drummer's name was Baldur, and he told Olly he'd been dating Þórhildur for about two weeks.

'She's so great! She's kind and funny and I love it when she sings in the shower. Do you have a girlfriend?'

Olly looked at the last slice of pizza in front of him and puffed out his cheeks.

'Well, my song was about someone, yeah,' he said eventually.

'Is that who you're travelling with around Iceland?'

'I wish! No, I'm here with my… er, I'm here on a work thing.'

'Who do you work for, Ol?' Baldur slurred, tipping back the last of his bottle of beer.

'Oh, you know… freelance.'

'Cool. Music?'

'Photography, actually.' Olly pulled his phone out of his pocket to show Baldur some of the shots he'd taken in Iceland, including the ones of the northern lights he'd transferred from his dad's camera.

'These are great; you should upload them to a stock image company I know, I bet they'd sell,' Baldur said approvingly.

'Maybe…'

'Hey Þórhildur, Ol's a photographer as well as a singer and a composer! He should talk to your brother.'

Þórhildur flashed Baldur a beautiful smile. Olly noticed her eyes matched her sweater and reminded him of his mother's.

'Well, Grímur's coming home tonight, so that can easily be arranged. He's just finished a tour of America,' she added.

'Is he, like, in a band?' Olly asked.

'No, he's the manager of a band, though. A really cool one. He manages all kinds of creative people. You know, like, he helps them get their careers going.'

Þórhildur looked at him with her head on one side.

'He'd really like you, Ol. Why don't you come back to Siglufjörður with us and meet him? We can give you a ride back early tomorrow morning.'

'Is it far?'

'Right at the top, you know, north of Akureyri, close to the arctic circle.' She drew a map with her finger in the air, and pointed to somewhere above her head. 'It's where they filmed that TV show, Trapped.'

Olly loved that these people had just accepted him, that they hadn't asked how old he was, or where he was studying, or judged his appearance. They hadn't hesitated to invite him to join them and now here they were wanting to introduce him to Þórhildur's brother Grímur, someone who knew what it took to be a successful artist.

'OK, sure. Thanks. Takk.'

31

'Tess, is that you?'

'It's me, yes.'

'I just wanted to say I'm sorry.'

'What for?'

'For being such a shit partner, parent, you name it.'

'What makes you say that Sean? It's a bit out of character for you.'

'I dunno, I just feel like I'm always fucking things up for you and Olly.'

'In what way? Is this drinker's remorse I'm hearing?' Tess sounded guarded but curious. She was at least listening, inviting him to expand on his opening statement.

'That too. You know, it's like… aargh, you know, I never seem to know how to make things right.'

'Well, it's like they say, you don't get a rehearsal when it comes to kids.'

'Or marriage.'

'True. Marriage is tough.'

'But strong, right? Ours, I mean.'

'We'll get through it.'

'Is that how you see it, that we just need to 'get through it'? Doesn't sound like much fun.'

'I agree, when you put it like that.'

'They were your words, Tess, not mine.'

'Hmmm. Look, I'm really tired and I've got stuff to do, can we do this another time?'

'Do what?'

'Whatever 'this' is. Sounds to me like you've been drinking, Sean.'

'Believe me: I'm stone cold sober, Tess. Have been for two days now. Planning to stay that way.'

'That's what you always say.'

'Look Tess, what the fuck's going on? Anton told me he's still in love with you, and that you'd… done something you both regretted. I think I know what he was getting at, but I need to hear it from you. I need to hear it from my wife.' Sean's voice wobbled as he finished speaking, and a strange, anguished tremor passed through his body.

'The thing is…' Tess began and then sighed. Sean could tell she had Radio 4 on in the background, because he could hear the beeps just before the nine o'clock news.

'Sean, I'm pregnant.'

32

Baldur drove off, somewhat unsteadily, in a battered Volvo along the road where Olly's dad had jumped the red light earlier that evening. Þórhildur was in the front seat texting her brother, and Olly sat in the back with his backpack on his lap, wondering if he'd made the right decision. He thought about asking Þórhildur if he could use her phone to text his dad, but that would mean explaining his circumstances in more detail, plus it would also run the risk of his father showing up at Þórhildur's house in Siglufjörður in the dead of night. He didn't want to experience a repeat of the disastrous police station episode at 3am. Anyhow, chances were, his dad was already fast asleep, so if Olly could find a way to get back to Akureyri before breakfast time tomorrow – if he just showed up at the Airbnb with a double espresso – his dad would never even need to know he'd been out all night. It was not as if he was doing anything illegal. Plus, Akureyri was a long way behind them now, so it was too late to ask Baldur to turn back. Olly could make out dark brooding mountains to his left and a vast expanse of water to their right. Þórhildur fiddled with the radio, just catching the end of a weather forecast.

'They say it's going to snow later tonight. It's already sub-zero. Are you warm enough back there, Ol? Baldur's car is such an old lady, the heating's stopped working. But there's a blanket on the backseat. Help yourself,' Þórhildur suggested, leaning over to tug the blanket out from under Baldur's cymbals. The cymbals shot forwards and slammed into the back of Baldur's seat, dropping to the floor with a loud clang.

'Hey, Þórhildur, watch what you're doing!'

But Baldur wasn't watching what he was doing either, and suddenly the car veered off the icy road and rolled over and over in slow motion onto the rough grass, finally slamming into a massive boulder, which flipped the vehicle back onto its wheels and left it a shuddering wreck, the engine still running.

There was a long pause, like when the TV loses its wifi signal in the middle of watching a film and goes into suspended animation.

The first flakes of snow started twirling down from the sky as Olly, jolted and confused, attempted to open the rear passenger door, but the child lock had been left on. Þórhildur murmured something, but Olly couldn't hear because of the loud static coming from the radio. When he glanced over at Baldur, he noticed a trickle of blood running down his forehead from beneath his beanie hat. He must have hit his head when he rolled the car.

Painfully slowly, Olly managed to climb over the back seat into the boot and find the button to open the tailgate from inside, just as a huge lorry thundered past, jabbing his face with icy shards. He groped his way round to the driver's door and wrenched it open. He had to lean against it to keep it open because the car was tipped back slightly which made the door want to fall shut.

'Baldur?' he whispered, tapping his shoulder. There was no response. 'Þórhildur, are you OK? I think Baldur is hurt.'

She looked confused for a moment, as if she didn't recognise Olly.

'Oh my god, oh my god…' she panted finally, holding her hands over her face when she turned and saw Baldur was injured and unconscious.

Olly was shaking uncontrollably in his parka as the wind whipped round him and his brain scrambled back and forth over what just happened. He realised he had no idea what you're supposed to do in these situations. Sol would know what to do, what to say. If Olly could just summon Sol's calm, soothing voice right now, everything would be OK. It was Sol's words that somehow got him through the day his dismal 'A' level results came out. Sol's assertive speech that had convinced him he didn't have to live up to his parents' expectations, only his own. That he could define his own agenda, speak his own truth, take control of his own life.

'Þórhildur, can you drive?' Olly asked.

'No. I can't.'

'I think we need to take Baldur to hospital, do you have your phone?'

'Yes. Wait a minute.' She pulled it out of her bag and handed it to him.

'Can you call for an ambulance? I don't know what number to dial.'

'Number? Whose number?'

'OK, don't worry, just unlock your phone for me, can you?'

'Unlock?'

'Yes, unlock. Please Þórhildur, hurry!'

He took the phone back and found himself dialling home.

He waited a long time for an answer.

'Hello? Who is this calling? It's very late, you know.'

'Mum? It's me.'

'Olly? What on earth's the matter?'

'Erm, we need an ambulance.'

'What's happened? Is your dad OK? He sounded very weird when I spoke to him earlier.'

'Look it's not Dad that's hurt, it's a friend. I was in his car. Please Mum, you need to help us. Can you phone Iceland's emergency services and get us an ambulance?'

'Where are you, darling? Whose car are you in? I thought you were with your dad!'

'It doesn't matter whose car. We just need to get him to hospital. He's not moving.'

'Did you have an accident?'

'He drove off the road, yes.'

'What road?'

'I don't know. The one that goes north from Akureyri. It goes to the place where they filmed that TV show.'

'Trapped?'

'Yeah.'

'Look darling, the best thing I can do is phone your dad and get him to come. Just wait there.'

'Please Mum, just call us an ambulance! Mum?'

He looked down at the phone and realised she'd hung up.

33

For the next hour, Sean wandered around Akureyri in a daze. He'd heard Tess say the word but could not connect it to the reality of – what? Conception? The months of gestation that lay ahead? No, that wasn't the issue at all. It was that sinking feeling when you finally get what you've always wanted, only to find that you don't actually want it anymore. Worse still, you know for a fact that the other person responsible for this new turn of events probably never wanted it in the first place. Another child, that is. But there it was, the stark fact, the blue line, the little shrimp, whoever it was.

Finally, his resistance totally worn down, he walked into a bar tormentingly called 'The Midas Rooms' and against his better judgement as well as doctor's orders, ordered a double vodka. He sat down at a table, pushing around the remains of two ice cubes that someone had spilled, as the barman cleared up around him. The place was almost empty, and seeing a battered guitar someone had left on the stage, Sean felt similarly abandoned, like he'd missed something important, and it was all over.

He noticed a scrap of paper on the floor and leaned down to pick it up. It had a poem scrawled on it called 'True North' which reminded him of the words Olly had sung when they were hanging out in the concrete sculpture. Come to think of it, the handwriting was also similar to Olly's. The opening lines seemed particularly apt to him right now:

> *Darkness flows in silent hollows*
> *Encircling my fear*

They described precisely the tangled mush inside his head as the vodka got to work on it – rather quickly since he had an empty stomach. He ordered another double in an attempt to make the judgemental, disappointed voice in his head go away, and then sat there, caught in a weird delirious limbo that was being kept in play by a combination of self-pity and self-loathing, the usual routine when he fell off the wagon. He pictured Tess in bed at home lying back against their navy-blue pillows, no doubt feeling nauseous due to what was growing inside her. He'd never asked her how far gone she was. Not that it mattered. He remembered Olly's arrival, this taut little face smeared with God knows what, all gums blazing. How had that helpless little thing, who became a robust toddler, 'a delightful child', so teachers said at every parents' evening, now become helpless once again, caught in the vice of mental illness? Sean decided there and then that he was recommitting to help Olly find a way out of wherever it was he'd got lost, and that before they left Iceland, he'd prove to himself and to Tess that he had the makings of being a good father, albeit a much older, much more decrepit one, to their second child.

Sean's phone buzzed in his pocket, but he wasn't in the mood to speak to anyone, so he ignored it. It buzzed several more times and then went silent.

'We're closing now, Sir, could you settle up your tab?'

He fished his credit card from his wallet but for some reason it was declined. So, he rummaged around in his pockets for some króna and came up short, blaming it on Olly who'd gone off with half his cash. He emerged from the bar, too drunk to remember the way back to their apartment and spent the next hour meandering through the streets until he finally found it.

Later, still in his jeans' pocket while he slept off his drunken stupor in the double bed, Sean's phone received six more missed calls: four from Tess, one from Anton and one from Sigríður.

34

Olly's arms ached from manoeuvring the barely conscious Baldur into the back of the Volvo, where Þórhildur was now cradling his head in her lap on the back seat and weeping. Olly slid into the driving seat and moved it backwards and forwards until he was the right distance from the pedals, just like his driving instructor had taught him. He switched off the radio, put on his seatbelt, and revved the engine, wondering how serious a crime it was to drive a car on the highway without a licence in Iceland.

Despite having rolled several times, somehow the old lady was still willing, and as Olly pressed the accelerator, the car edged forwards, grinding and bumping over the rough, frozen grass as he steered it back towards the road.

He'd never driven in the dark before; that time he moved their SUV didn't really count because he hadn't had to deal with any traffic. Thankfully the Volvo was an automatic and felt quite similar to their SUV to drive; Olly just hoped he wouldn't need to do anything too complicated.

'Sorry, we're going over a bump now,' he called out, willing the car to mount the slight rise at the verge of the road, and Baldur groaned as the Volvo bounced back onto the smooth tarmac.

'Do you know what you're doing, Olly?' Þórhildur whimpered.

'Not really. Do you know the way to the hospital?'

'Just head for Akureyri. There's an Emergency Department there.'

Olly drove on, trying not to look into the headlights of the oncoming cars, trying not to think about what just happened, trying not to cry. He swallowed hard, concentrating on the memory of that beaker of glacier water. So much for it being the cure to everything. There were clearly no magic potions in real life.

35

Starving and totally shattered, Olly walked out of the hospital and realised it was now dawn, the south-eastern horizon banded with orange and pink. Zipping up his parka, he tried to get his bearings, but there were no landmarks he recognised. He stopped someone in the hospital car park to ask the way downtown.

'Just go past the cathedral and it's a little further,' the man assured him in a thick Icelandic accent.

The wind was biting through his clothes, as he hunched down inside his hood, half wishing he'd stayed in the warmth of the emergency room, where Þórhildur was waiting for Baldur to be X-rayed. But she insisted Olly went to get some breakfast, even offering him the car keys in case he wanted to drive around in the Volvo until he found some.

He stopped at a cafe and found he had just enough króna left to buy his father a single espresso. Olly wrapped both hands around the paper cup to retain its warmth as he walked down the street. When he finally reached the steel-grey front door to their Airbnb apartment, he hesitated before knocking, aware that he had not rehearsed what he was going to say to explain his ten-hour absence to his father.

Hearing Sean's footsteps in the hallway, Olly could tell immediately – just by the erratic rhythm– that he'd been drinking. He heard his dad clear his throat, and, as the lock turned and the door swung open, Sean's bleary gaze told Olly all he needed to know. His father was pissed. He'd managed to stay off the booze for all of forty-eight hours.

'I bought you a coffee,' Olly mumbled through chapped lips. And then, out of nowhere, something in his over-tired brain suddenly flipped, just like the moment Baldur's car swerved off the road. Without thinking, he flung the cup at his father's chest. The plastic lid flew off and hot, black liquid shot everywhere. Sean gasped and clutched at the steaming patch on the front of his white T-shirt. Instantly provoked, he swung for Olly and clouted his left ear. As the boy fell sideways from the force of the blow, Sean loomed towards his child and raised his arm to strike again. Olly was trying desperately to roll onto his side, but the best he could do to stop his father's punches from raining down onto his head was to wrap his arms around his face. Sean was tiring fast, and threw one final, inebriated blow that missed Olly's body completely and assaulted the pavement instead.

Nursing his fist, Sean stared down at his son's face lying in the gutter, smeared with blood. Something about Olly's stunned expression – the narrowed, wounded eyes and dusty grey complexion – reminded Sean of a traumatised young soldier he'd once had to shoot for National Geographic.

'What the hell?' Sean slurred, taking a step backwards. A small crowd had gathered on the opposite pavement, their faces horrified and incredulous, wondering what would happen next and whether they should intervene to prevent further injury.

'Yeah, Dad, what the hell?' Olly erupted as he struggled back onto his feet, clutching his bloody ear. 'What the fuck is wrong with you? You're out of your mind! You're always making me feel like there's something wrong with me, but you're the one who's got a problem. You're an alcoholic who's too deluded to admit what's really going on. You haven't got a clue, have you? Mum tries her best even though you don't deserve it, but you never put either her or me first, you never even try to see things from our point of view, you never…' Olly was sobbing by this point, as Sean stared in disbelief, shaking his head.

Olly pushed past him into the hallway of the apartment, stumbling over his father's walking boots as he ran into his room and slammed the door. Sean heard him drag a chair across the room and jam it under the handle. Then the dull thump of his child dropping like a stone onto the bed and the muffled animal-like sound he made as he screamed into his pillow.

36

Sean woke to the sound of someone hammering on the front door. At first his brain turned it into a mallet pounding a fencepost into the frozen ground in his dream, but then the sound of Sigga's urgent voice brought him out of his slumber and onto his feet. Didn't he just do this – open the door to someone else – like, half an hour ago? Had he lost all track of time? A weird vision of his son's bloodied face clouded his mind, but he dismissed it as another drink-induced nightmare he'd had.

Sigga was standing, hands on hips, in an oversized Icelandic cardigan, with Roman tugging at her elbow.

'Where's Olly? Is he hurt? Is he safe?' she said with a hardened edge of concern in her voice.

'I dunno,' Sean mumbled, as the smell of coffee on his T-shirt jogged his memory about his son's melodramatic outburst earlier that morning. Or was it afternoon? He scratched his head, and, too addled to say anything else, he gestured for them both to come inside with a caricatured sweep of his arm.

Sigga wasted no time brewing some fresh coffee and finding a packet of biscuits in the welcome pack the owners had left for them. Handing a biscuit to Roman and sitting him down on the sofa next to her, she pushed wisps of hair away from her face and sighed.

'This has got to stop, Sean.'

'Our trip? We've got another week to go, I've still got the Westfjords and Snæfellsnes to cover.'

'Of course I don't mean your work, Sean. This is much more important. I mean your drinking, your complete dereliction of duty when it comes to your own child's wellbeing, and your narcissistic pretence that you're never in the wrong.'

Sean had never heard his former boss speak so plainly to him before, never seen this sterner side of Sigríður, not even during the most stressful periods of working for her at *National Geographic*.

'Sigga, come on, let's not make a mountain out of everything, please…' he stammered from the other side of the coffee table.

'The only mountain we're dealing with here is entirely of your own making, Sean. I had your poor wife ringing me in the dead of night, out of her mind about both of you, something she shouldn't be having to deal with in her condition. Why didn't you tell me you were expecting a child, Sean? I'm thrilled for all of you, especially Olly. When I saw him playing with Roman, I couldn't help thinking what a wonderful brother he would make, so I can't understand why you didn't mention it.'

'It's because I didn't know. That's God's honest truth, Sigga. I didn't fucking know,' his fist hammered the coffee table to emphasise his point. 'Not until last night.'

Sigga frowned, either at his choice of expletive or because she didn't believe him. She closed her eyes and kissed the top of Roman's head, pulling him close to her.

'I think you should come and stay with us for a couple of days, just until everything is on a more even keel, Sean,' she said slowly.

'Are you inviting me, or are you telling me?'

'I'm asking you. As a friend. I think you need a time out. You need to reflect on what's really going on here, but first, you need to dry out.'

Sean nodded. But he felt cornered.

Olly appeared in the doorway, his face swollen, bloody and tearstained.

'Oh. I heard voices.'

'Olly!' Roman cried, rushing across and wrapping his arms around Olly's legs. Sigga turned and looked aghast.

'Oh my God, you poor child! What on earth happened to you?' Sigga rushed across the room and gently led Olly to the sofa, where she set about cleaning his cuts and bruises with the first aid kid she'd brought with her. Sean walked away, cracking out his aching knuckles and lobbing a dismissive order at his son.

'Apparently, we're going to spend a couple more days in Húsavík, Olly. Pack your bags.'

Sigga gave her former employee a searching, exasperated look at the same moment that Roman burst into floods of tears.

37

Olly was in the garden shed, curled up on a pile of old blankets with Apollo, absently scrolling through old messages on his phone, when Sigga found him.

'Hæ. There you are! Your face looks a bit better. Listen Olly, your father needs to spend a bit of time by himself at the house, so I was thinking, how about you, me and Roman check out the Astronaut Monument and the Museum of Exploration?'

Olly was silent for a moment. He liked Sigga and he knew she was trying to be kind and helpful, but he was feeling so down, he couldn't cope with the idea of leaving the shed, let alone looking round a museum.

'Is the museum about the Apollo mission thing that happened in Iceland?' he asked in a monotone.

'Yes, it most certainly is. Neil Armstrong himself came here in the late 60s, when I was little, to train in the Highlands for the arduous task of taking rock samples on the Moon. It's Roman's favourite place to go on a rainy afternoon.'

'I guess. If Roman wants to go.'

Shuffling, Olly followed her reluctantly back up the garden path into the house, his shoelaces undone.

Roman, who was already dressed up for the occasion in a silver snowsuit and ski mittens, thrust the spaceman from his windowsill into Olly's hand as soon as he entered the kitchen, and dragged him towards the front door.

They drove in Sigga's Land Rover round to the other side of the harbour and pulled up not far from the monument, which turned out to be a dull stone plaque outside a boring-looking building.

'Is that it?' Olly remarked. Roman traced his forefinger line by line over the names inscribed on the monument. There were two lists, one lot of astronauts who came in 1965 and a second group in 1967, the year Olly's dad was born.

To a Londoner like Olly, who was used to school trips to the Science Museum and the V&A, using the word museum was a gross exaggeration, this one being no more than a couple of rooms of framed black and white photographs, some glass cabinets containing pieces of rock, and a replica NASA spacesuit. Roman pointed out several features on this exhibit that differed from his mini figure's outfit, including the colour of the space boots, and Olly's dark mood lifted somewhat when the little boy recited from memory the famous Armstrong quote printed on a plaque beside a 3D model of his Moon landing footprint:

'One thmall thtep for man, one giant leap for mankind!' Roman lisped in halting English, then proceeded to do giant leaps all around the small museum, until Olly couldn't help but laugh.

Having seen everything there was to see, Sigga and Olly walked out of the museum swinging Roman between them. Olly remembered his parents doing the same thing with him when he was little. Roman squealed with delight and then ran back to the Land Rover.

'Where are Roman's parents?' Olly asked Sigga, when they got back in the vehicle. She glanced over her shoulder to look at Roman who was falling asleep on the back seat and then lowered her voice to reply.

'Well, his mother – my daughter Katla – is doing a PhD in Boston.

And his Daddy died in a tragic accident when Roman was three.'

'Oh. Does he still remember his dad?'

'I show Roman photographs of him, and he sometimes asks about him. His dad has a brother – Uncle Magnus – who's been very good to Roman. But he lives in England, so Roman doesn't see him that often. It's so sad, my son-in-law was a wonderful man; Katla was devastated when he died.'

'Was he Icelandic?'

'No, he was British, like your dad.'

'And does Roman have any brothers or sisters?'

'No, he's an only child,' Sigga replied, then after a pause added, 'Just like you.'

38

Pacing up and down in his dressing gown in Sigga's kitchen like a caged lion, Sean couldn't find a way to settle. His thoughts were ducking and diving all over the place, and there was nothing he could do except move his body around too. At intervals, he stopped to crack his knuckles and scream, 'Jesus, what the fuck have I done to deserve this?'

Finally, his stuck record stopped when he felt his phone buzz in his jeans pocket.

'David, hi.' Sean tried his best to switch to a tone of voice that was more business-like and professional, but his voice came out raw and ragged from all the manic shouting.

'No, wait, listen, I...

...Look, I don't think you're being very fair, David.

...OK, if that's the way it is, I'll email you my resignation this afternoon. But you'll be hearing from my lawyer. This is constructive dismissal.'

The call ended and Sean stared at the screen.

'Tosser!' he yelled, throwing the phone onto the kitchen table with such force it skidded onto the floor and landed next to the bin. As he bent down to pick it up, he saw the phone was now covered in pink glitter and felt momentarily chastened. He sat down heavily on the kitchen stool and stared in total disbelief at the cracked screen as well as a long list of missed calls from the previous day. Frowning, he tried calling Tess back, but it went straight to voicemail.

'Tess, honey, do me a favour: fuck off!' he shouted into the phone.

He needed a drink and started rifling through the kitchen cupboards for a bottle of something – anything. When it eluded him, he started throwing crockery and tossing aside jars of jam and pickles in a wild fury, which smashed and spilled all over the kitchen floor. Finally, he found a half bottle of brandy next to Sigga's tub of baking powder and took a good long swig.

Seething with frustration and having no other outlet, Sean tapped on Anton's number, since he too appeared to have called him the previous night. Anton's deep voice reverberated around the kitchen.

'Sean! What's the story? Been trying to get hold of you. I wanted to ask you something.'

'Was it about me hitting Olly? Because if it was, it's none of your fucking business.'

'No, it wasn't. I have a proposition for you.'

'Seriously? I thought it was only my wife you 'propositioned'. But if you want to press charges for the black eye I gave you, be my guest. I'll see you in court…'

'Hang on, Sean, you're jumping to conclusions. I'm all for letting bygones be bygones. I once gave you a black eye, if I recall correctly?'

'You did indeed. You hot-headed bastard.'

'Pot calling the kettle black there, mate.'

'OK, so what's the big idea?'

'I'm done with horse-riding. None of the bloody nags here is any good. And Ólafur isn't keen on accompanying me on what he calls my 'Mad Quest'. So, I'm asking you to come instead.'

'What 'Mad Quest' are you referring to?'

'Well, it was you who gave me the idea, actually. Before you got blind drunk and gave me the black eye, you mentioned that you'd always wanted to experience Iceland's interior – you know, drive into the Highlands. I admit the roads are a bit icy, but technically they're still open, and here we both are, two blokes having a mid-life crisis in Iceland, so why not join me? I'm driving my sports car on the dirt road over to Askja early tomorrow morning. Apparently, the view of the caldera from the rim of the volcano is divine. I'm also planning to go skinny-dipping – Ólafur says Lake Víti is a pleasant twenty-odd degrees, sometimes even warmer, so basically it's the world's most remote jacuzzi. It'll be like wallowing in second heaven. Be a devil, meet me there!'

Sean could hear Sigga's Land Rover pulling up outside. He had that cornered feeling again.

'OK, I'll come. Text me the co-ordinates.'

39

'Did your father say where he was going this morning, Olly? The SUV is not in the drive,' Sigga informed him when he came down to breakfast. She was still cleaning up the kitchen after his father's alcohol-deprived tantrum the day before.

'No, he didn't say.'

'Never mind. Maybe he went to fill up with petrol or something. There's muesli and fruit on the table love, help yourself. I'll be out in the greenhouse.'

'How much longer is Roman, you know, on his machine?'

'Just for another half an hour. I'll bring him down after that.'

Olly got himself a bowl of muesli and a glass of juice from the fridge and sat down at the table. There was an Icelandic newspaper lying next to him with a picture of bright orange lava rolling down a hillside. The caption underneath said 'Geldingadalir'. Olly stared at the article in Icelandic, trying to work out if it said a volcano had just started erupting. He turned the pages and stopped on the one where Sigga had been doing a sudoku puzzle. He finished it in his head and then looked at the crossword clues, but it was impossible to figure out Icelandic. It looked much harder than Polish. And Spanish. That made him remember his appalling exam results again and his mood instantly slipped down a notch.

These days he could calibrate his depression according to how his body responded in the mornings, with the 'can't-even-get-out-of-bed' feeling being a deflated one. Today was about a three, he decided. Better than the last couple of days, which clocked in barely above zero, hardly surprising after being beaten up for no good reason by his own father. At least today he was up, eating something, and had already managed to have some sort of conversation with Sigga. Any day he saw Sol had always been either a nine or a ten, apart from the night they got arrested, when it went into negative numbers on the spot. Singing in The Midas Rooms had rated as a solid seven-and-a-half, but was now ruined by what happened afterwards, which brought it down to about a two. If a week or so went by and he didn't drop below a five, it was a sign things were starting to look up, but that hadn't happened for a while. A consistent three/four was more typical. He wondered if other people with depression measured their symptoms in this way, and if Anton could relate to this if Olly were to ask him. He wondered if Anton had gone horse-riding without him the other day, or if he was back in England now, doing whatever rich people do when they aren't on holiday.

He heard a car pull up in the drive and went to let his father in. When he opened the front door, he was surprised to find a familiar Volvo standing there. Baldur and Þórhildur got out of the car, smiling and carrying some kind of present. Olly waved but failed to smile back.

'How did you know I was here?' he asked.

'Iceland's a small place, it's not too difficult,' Þórhildur said winking at him. 'Here, this is for you, to say thank you for helping Baldur and me. What you did was very brave and very cool.'

He took the present and walked back into the kitchen.

'Sigga will be back in a minute; I don't know how to work the coffee machine,' he mumbled.

'Aren't you going to open it, Ol?'

'Oh. OK.' He slowly peeled away the paper and inside was a box containing an orange effects pedal for a guitar.

'It's a vintage one that Grímur was getting rid of, but it makes the most awesome distortions,' Baldur enthused, 'We figured you might like it, since you said you were into them.'

'Thanks, that's a great present.' Olly was aware that the flatness in his voice didn't match the content of his words, and there was an uncomfortably long silence.

'What happened after you left the hospital, Ol? Why are you back in Húsavík, I thought you were heading to the Western Fjords next?' Þórhildur asked eventually, when it was clear Olly was at a loss what to say.

'My Dad got sacked yesterday. And my Mum just told him she's pregnant.'

'Oh my goodness! That's... um. And what happened to your ear?'

Olly reached up to touch the surgical dressing which Sigga had put there.

'It's just... a cut. How's your head, Baldur?' Olly asked.

'The scans came back OK, no permanent damage, thankfully.'

Sigga came in from the garden.

'Oh, you didn't tell me you were having friends over, Olly. Are you going to introduce me?'

Olly was having trouble knowing what to say, so Þórhildur jumped in quickly.

'Hi, I'm Þórhildur and this is Baldur.'

'Ah, so you're the couple whose Volvo Olly drove back to Akureyri!'

'That's us.'

It seemed funny to Olly that they were all speaking English in front of him when they would normally talk to each other in Icelandic, and it made him feel really awkward, so he disappeared upstairs to see if Roman was ready to come down. When he was halfway up the stairs, the landline started ringing, a loud insistent bell tone coming from the living room. Sigga went to answer it.

'Sean? Where are you?'

Olly strained to listen. Sigga sounded serious.

'Jesus Christ! OK, listen, don't panic, just stay put and I'll alert the ranger to send out a rescue team.'

Olly heard her put the phone down and waited. Sigga came upstairs and went into Roman's room, Olly following after her. She disconnected the dialysis machine and helped Roman out of bed, then when he'd run off to use the bathroom, she slumped in the armchair, deep in thought.

'What's happened?' Olly asked her, his voice all quivery.

'Your father's driven off into the Highlands, without submitting a travel plan online, with no food or water, to meet up with some friend of his called Anton, and he's called me in a panic because this Anton guy has apparently fallen down a ravine or got lost in a snowdrift or something. Along with Sean's precious camera, by the sounds of it. You couldn't make it up.'

Þórhildur, hearing the emotion in Sigga's voice, had come upstairs and put her head around the door.

'I should have known he was up to something when I found all that mess in the kitchen yesterday!' Sigga groaned. 'I ask you: who assaults their own child, abuses people's goodwill, refuses to admit they've got a problem, and then takes off like this? He's totally out of his mind.'

'Should we call the air ambulance?' Þórhildur suggested.

'We could, but the trouble is, Sean's got no idea where they are. It's blizzard conditions up there by the sound of it.'

'So, what are you going to do?' Olly whispered.

'I'm going to have to look for them myself.'

Sigga started gathering items she might need from various drawers and cupboards – a head torch, ski mittens, a satellite phone, some rope. She threw everything into a blue Ikea bag and walked back into the kitchen to fill up some stainless-steel bottles with water.

'Þórhildur, is there any chance you and Baldur could mind Roman for me while Olly and I go to Askja? Oh, and I also need you to register my trip on the government website, is that OK?'

'Of course. We'll hang out here til you get back.'

'Thank you, he'll be good as gold, always is. Now Olly, get your things.'

'You want me to come too?'

'Yes, of course, I need you.'

Olly remembered how his dad had berated him for his navigation skills, and how he'd said more than once that they would not be visiting Iceland's perilous inland wilderness, full of glaciers and volcanoes and no real roads. He tried to imagine Anton stranded somewhere, up to his neck in snow. Suddenly, Baldur's car accident and Olly's heroic rescue mission to get him to hospital seemed insignificant. The crazy punch-up with his father after he'd thrown coffee at him and the way they had been avoiding each other ever since also now seemed utterly stupid. As usual, he felt in some way responsible for his dad's predicament, as if he had caused it. And underneath that feeling of guilt and inadequacy was an overwhelming need to be reunited with his father, no matter what.

Roman was standing at the front door, waiting to wave them off. Olly wondered what Apollo was up to, expecting him to bark goodbye too.

'Uncle Sean OK,' the little boy assured him, and pressed the spaceman figure into Olly's hand for luck.

40

Sean clicked on the co-ordinates Anton had texted him the night before and zoomed in on the circular red marker. It was planted in the middle of a turquoise crater next to a much larger expanse of blue water, which he knew was Lake Askja, the second deepest in Iceland, occupying the volcano's caldera. Apart from grey arctic tundra stretching for hundreds of kilometres in all directions, the only signs of civilisation visible on satellite view were a handful of huts at the end of the F88 'road', which constituted a place called Dreki. In his head a litany of Tess's favourite epithets was running like a tickertape on repeat: You irresponsible maniac. You selfish bastard. You utter idiot.

But something had got hold of him now, and he felt compelled to go. If Anton was up for it, so was he. Anton was always doing crazy things, and nothing bad had ever come of it. What's more, no one ever tried to talk him out of it. He was rich and free in a way Sean envied. But Anton wasn't one of those rich men who hoarded their wealth and became all self-righteous and dull. No, Anton used his money to squeeze the juice out of life. To seek out its thrills and chills. The Icelandic Highlands were a once-in-a-lifetime experience, as Anton rightly said the other night. Sean dialled up the volume on Anton's cavalier style of commentary to drown out his wife's insults: Do it while you still can. Be your own man for once. Who cares what anyone thinks?

He took another swig from Sigga's brandy bottle, turned off his bedside light and crept out onto the landing. It was still dark outside, no sign of dawn yet. Through the open door to Roman's room, Sean saw a shadow cast by the moon shining on the planetary mobile hanging from the ceiling and watched for a moment as Saturn orbited slowly past Jupiter. Apollo yawned and stretched and got up to greet him, tail wagging. He could see another heap on Roman's floor next to where the dog had been lying and realised it was his son. Olly must have moved his mattress into Roman's room to keep him company. Or maybe it was Olly who needed company or, more likely, to avoid sharing a bedroom with his violent, unpredictable father. As Sean recalled Olly lying on the pavement in Akureyri, he felt a tiny prick of conscience but quickly pushed it away. The dog followed him downstairs, getting excited at the prospect of an early morning walk.

In the end, Sean had no choice but to let Apollo come with him, knowing he'd just bark and wake everyone up if he left him shut in behind the front door.

41

Wishing he'd had something to eat before leaving, Sean thundered east back along Route One. At this hour in the morning, there were no other vehicles on the lonely stretch of highway. He whistled tunelessly in an effort to control his erratic breathing and waited for the sat nav to announce the turning for the F88 coming up on the right.

When he finally reached the junction, a sign said 'Askja 100km' and there was a small lay-by with various maps covered in red and yellow warning notices, all spelling out the dangers of going into the interior unprepared. Sean inwardly scoffed at the hordes of cautious tourists who had doubtless stopped to read them before continuing west to Mývatn in their puny hired hatchbacks, deciding that Askja was just too far and the hazards of driving along the F88 were not for the likes of them.

But here he was. No turning back.

After just a few kilometres down the rough gravel track that was F88 and countless expletives, Sean knew what the F stood for. But Askja, with its strange boxy shape silhouetted against the dawn sky in the distance, dominated this vast inland plain with its snow-tipped promise and lured Sean on.

As he came to the first ford, where the water was moving quickly, carrying floes of ice, there was another warning signing stressing the importance of judging the depth of the water and waiting for a second vehicle to undertake the crossing together. He slowed down and glanced over his shoulder, as if checking to see if someone was looking, before accelerating the SUV, and with a little tyre skid, plunged into the river, willing the vehicle to make it across.

Sean felt triumphant as the vehicle lurched back out onto the dirt track on the other side, the engine still chugging, and celebrated by swallowing the last of the brandy. Tess's voice whispered very quietly, Dutch Courage. He wondered briefly what the English had against the Dutch to adopt this turn of phrase. For the next few miles, he idly pondered other drinking idioms: to drink someone under the table, to drink like a fish, a stiff drink, and the one he'd recently been accused of by both Sigga and David: you can lead a horse to water, but you can't make it drink. Had he been fired for his stubbornness? For his sheer, blatant, bloody-minded obstinacy? Or because he was a bad photographer? Had he lost his edge? Sean shot a quick glance onto the backseat to make sure his camera bag was still there. He got quite a shock when he caught sight of the dog, snoozing on his thermal coat, having already forgotten that he'd brought Apollo with him.

About halfway there, when the odometer had added another fifty kilometres but Askja's weird boxy profile didn't look any closer at all, Sean stopped. All his limbs were tingling and jittery from the bumpy road. He was getting a headache from constantly squinting into the morning sun, and cursed the fact that he couldn't find his Raybans. As he stepped down from the SUV, Apollo jumped out too, and they both stood on the grey lunar surface, stretching and shivering.

The sky to the south was clear, thin bands of cloud like taut stretchmarks reaching from east to west, but from the north, Sean could see ominous snow clouds moving in, dark zeppelins which he knew from experience made for spectacular photography but were harbingers of doom. He went back for his camera and his coat and took a few handheld photos. The road was barely visible on any of them, since there was virtually nothing to distinguish it from the surrounding terrain other than being slightly smoother. Sean knew it was forbidden to drive off road anywhere in Iceland, but it was nevertheless very tempting to ignore the textural difference and take a shortcut. He pictured Anton speeding towards Dreki in his sports car, and wondered whether he would cut corners here and there, go off piste. It was the sort of thing Anton did. When Olly had called Sean out for using that idiom, he realised it was one he'd copied from Anton. In fact, Anton epitomised the notion of 'off-piste'.

He thought he could hear another vehicle rattling towards him in the distance and walked briskly back to the SUV. He didn't want to have to tailgate someone else all the way there. He'd rather have them in his rearview mirror.

For the next hour, Sean masked the noise of the road and the engine by tuning into a succession of crackly, indistinct radio stations. The voices and songs were all chopped up, like the dirty, pitted surface of a glacier. Over the top of this cacophony, his brain kept imagining he could hear Olly singing one continuous treble note without taking a single breath. Sean tried to push away the niggling feeling that he was neglecting his son's needs, putting his own irrational needs first. The only thing he was doing right on this trip was failing spectacularly. That, it seemed, was his perverse true north. Sean narrowed his eyes and trained them on the far horizon, pushing his shameful treatment of Olly angrily away. As the road curved abruptly to the left, he felt suddenly alive and alert, like a climax predator latching onto a scent, or a poacher determined to bring home a handsome trophy carcass.

Sean considered what epitomised the idea of a trophy for him, when had he last – literally or metaphorically – held one aloft and heard everyone cheer? Not since winning a house rugby in sixth form, probably. Meeting Tess on New Year's Day 2001 definitely ranked higher than the small hurrah when she said yes to marrying him. But, to his shame, there had been a much larger hurrah when he learned the contents of his old man's will, mainly because it enabled him to wipe out a dubious debt that Sean didn't want Tess to know about.

42

By the time Sean arrived in Dreki, the sinister snow clouds had rolled in. Seeing his partner in crime had finally arrived, Anton jumped out of his sports car and strolled across to Sean's SUV, stabbing the rough ground with a pair of those expensive hiking sticks and wearing a ridiculous multi-coloured Peruvian hat, complete with ear flaps and woolly tassels that was the same vivid purples and greens as his fading black eye.

'Good man. Thought you'd bailed.'

'It was a bloody long way; this better be worth it,' Sean replied.

'We're not quite there yet. Got to drive a bit further. Let's take your vehicle, mine's done. Useless low axle, almost didn't make it across one the fords.'

Pleasantries completed, Sean shoved Apollo into Anton's car, with the words 'Not your mission today, mate', then the two men climbed into Sean's vehicle and Anton directed him along another dirt road to an even bleaker, more elevated spot with a wooden shack housing two toilets and signposts marking the start of the hiking route to Lake Askja and Víti, the crater lake.

Víti looked like a beautiful turquoise pearl nestled in a small depression from this distance. They were surrounded by dark flanks of the Dyngjufjöll mountains, patches of snow clinging to the unrelenting grey basalt.

'They look like killer whales,' Sean said, pointing.

'What? Where?' Anton glanced around puzzled, looking for a large sea creature.

'The mountains, I mean.'

Anton touched the remains of his black eye and fell silent as they reached the parking place.

'I must say, I'm up for a bit of a hike, aren't you?' Sean enthused as he got out of the SUV. He stretched out his limbs and did a few push-ups against the side of the car for good measure. He was starting to feel something stronger than Dutch courage now, something along the lines of 'who dares wins', which was surging through his body in waves. Meanwhile Anton was still inside the SUV, stuffing his yellow satellite phone into his coat pocket and thumbing through the pages of his waterproof guidebook, as if hesitant to begin their expedition.

'Come on mate, there's only one way down; we're not going to need your damn book,' Sean joked, striding off past the wooden shack with his camera slung around his neck. He heard the car door slam and Anton's voice bouncing off the bare rock as he read aloud from the guidebook.

'It says that Askja's beautiful lake holds deadly secrets, you know. As one of Iceland's sleeping beauties, it's considered extremely dangerous and could erupt at any time, given recent movements in the magma underneath and the thinness of the Earth's crust in this location. In fact, two volcanologists disappeared without trace while investigating it back in 1907. They were never seen again, dead or alive…'

'Well, we've all got our deadly little secrets haven't we, Anton? Anyway, if people last went missing over a century ago, there's a good chance we'll get out alive before the next eruption. Come on, what's the matter? Lost your nerve?'

Of all the things Sean had been expecting to happen on this so-called 'Mad Quest', Anton chickening out was not one of them. He'd always regarded him to be a totally fearless – in fact a totally foolhardy – human being, always willing to step into the jaws of fate without a second thought. And yet here was Anton behaving as though he'd rather be at home watching TV. Anton's timidity on the brink of an adventure was having an emboldening effect on Sean's mood, making him impatient to get moving, to cut to the chase.

But this new balance of power was short-lived. Almost as soon as they got going, Sean found that the loose ashy gravel under foot kept giving way, and the light dusting of ice prevented him from gaining any traction. When the path started dropping downhill towards the crater, he became increasingly less sure of himself the steeper it became. While Sean's boots slipped and slithered, Anton, spiking the ground firmly with his fancy walking poles, slowly regained his composure as they descended the scree slope towards the vivid blue lake.

They were silent for a while, both men lost in thought as they picked their way in single file through the volcanic tuff, Sean in front.

'You spoken to Tess in the last couple of days?' Anton queried casually from behind.

'Yup.'

'Did you tell her I'd confessed to you about our little fling?'

Sean let out a small snort and glanced back.

'Is that what you call it?'

Anton turned up both palms nonchalantly as if to say, 'how else would you describe it?', then continued with his line of inquiry.

'She tell you about the baby?'

'You already know about the baby?' Sean blurted out, trying to keep his tone light despite feeling affronted that Tess had told Anton about the pregnancy before she'd seen fit to tell her own husband.

'Yes, stands to reason, don't you think? In the erm, circumstances.'

'What do you mean?'

'Well, when you punched me in the face the other night as soon as I mentioned that I'd slept with her once or twice lately, what I omitted to say was: there have been some unexpected consequences…'

'What do you mean: unexpected consequences?' But even as he posed the question, a shockwave of realisation ripped through Sean's gut, as if his spleen had just exploded. He bent over double, clutching his stomach and staring at the rocky ground, struggling to process this earth-shattering piece of information and contend with the volley of emotions it had fired up inside him. When Tess told him she was pregnant, like a naive idiot, he'd just assumed that it was his – that he, Sean Mackie, was naturally the father of the baby. But here was Anton, casually inferring something quite, quite different. A whole new species of anger erupted from the very core of Sean's impetuous being.

Anton strode on regardless of the impact his revelation was having on his walking buddy, calmly overtaking him as he spiked the ground with his walking poles at evenly spaced intervals like a well-oiled machine, his eyes trained on the opposite rim of the crater.

'I told your wife, if she wants to keep it, it's up to you and her.'

'Me? What the hell's it got to do with me if I'm not the father?' Sean growled.

'Technically the paternity issue is up for debate until we have a DNA test done once the kid is born. But whoever's baby it is, let's face it, you're probably a whole lot better at fatherhood than I would be. I'm just not the reliable type,' Anton replied airily.

'Excuse me?' Sean said, straightening up too quickly and feeling slightly faint. 'What makes you think I'm going to bring up your kid? Jesus, this is the most outrageous thing anyone has ever said to me!'

Sean was feeling insulted on so many levels he didn't know where to begin. Maybe he should start with the offensive back-handed compliment that Anton tossed out about him being more reliable.

'I suppose what I'm saying, given my own miserable childhood, is that I'm just not cut out for family life,' Anton clarified, waving a dismissive hand, 'Plus, us living together would never work, that's what I told Tess.'

'What do you mean, 'us' living together? You, me and Tess under one roof? Christ, what a thought!'

Sean picked up a loose rock and, aiming for Anton's head, lobbed it with all his might. Anton instinctively ducked as if it was a badly bowled cricket ball and calmly resumed his line of reasoning.

'No, of course I don't mean a *ménage à trois*, that would be frankly ridiculous. I mean Tess and me living together. We might have been meant for each other, but we weren't meant to be parents. So, I'll happily sign over the custody to the two of you.'

Anton made his unborn child sound like a poorly-conceived business start-up – no, worse than that – a deal he'd got going on the side that he'd grown tired of and was looking to offload. Sean's fingers were unconsciously balling up into fists, his shoulders squaring up inside his coat, and somewhere in the vicinity of his kidneys, he could tell his adrenal glands had set to work pumping out their magic juice.

'You're a total wanker, you know that don't you?' Sean said quietly through clenched teeth, but there was no response. 'Did you hear what I said, Anton?' he said, louder this time, his question emerging as a warm cloud from his mouth and hovering in the cold, clear air, as the words ricocheted back at him from the opposite side of the crater. 'I could kill you for this. You've ruined my marriage, you entitled bastard!'

'Sorry, I didn't quite catch that?' Anton said, lifting one of the flaps on his idiotic hat and turning his ear towards Sean. The whole gesture came across as deliberately mocking, but Sean had no idea whether Anton was trying to cause more offence or not. If he was, he was definitely succeeding.

'I SAID…' Sean stopped mid-sentence. The sight of Anton's self-satisfied expression and the tassels on his stupid hat flapping around in the wind made him suddenly feel overwhelmed with frustration and anger. Waiting for Sean to continue, Anton tucked both walking poles into the crook of one elbow to free up one hand so he could reach into his pocket. He pulled out a large white handkerchief and proceeded to blow his nose with infuriating affectation. It was the final straw.

Sean seized the moment and lunged forwards, grabbing hold of Anton in a clumsy rugby tackle. The two of them immediately over-balanced and skittered down the crater wall as one entity, rolling as they gathered momentum. Sean was determined not to let go, not even when he heard a sharp crack and realised that his camera had snagged on a rock.

'What are you trying to do, Sean? Kill us both?' Anton gasped, trying to wrest Sean's fierce grip from around his torso and managing to knee him in the groin. Sean was beside himself, pummelling Anton's chest, his fists repeatedly missing their mark as the two men came apart and catapulted down the rest of the slope in free fall.

As the side of the crater began to level out, Sean came to an abrupt halt a few feet from the water's edge, dusty, dazed and disorientated. While he lay on his back panting furiously, Anton leapt to his feet and immediately started peeling his layers off. Hopping on one leg and then the other, he removed his boots, trousers, pants and socks.

'What the hell are you doing?' Sean choked, incredulous.

'What does it look like? I'm going for a dip, like I told you. Not often you get to swim in a volcanic crater, is it? Plus, I'd say we both need to calm down after our little tussle!' Anton sniffed the sulphurous air, savouring the view. Then, naked apart from the Peruvian hat, he waded out into the water. Sean watched in silent disbelief as Anton lowered his body below the surface and began sculling towards the middle of the lake, where he floated on his back like an otter, surveying the splendour of this remote volcanic panorama as if nothing had happened between them.

Still seething and reeling from the shock of their violent altercation, Sean sat by the water's edge, hugging his knees and rocking backwards and forwards. He had no desire to join Anton for a swim despite his fondness for outdoor bathing and the invitingly warm water, mainly because he was having a hard time persuading his body's fight or flight response, now triggered and in full swing, to calm down. He felt as if the plumes of roiling magma that were bubbling up beneath this very crater might actually erupt from inside his own body. He could feel the heat of it, the intense pressure building in his skull, behind his eyes, throbbing in his ears and temples. At the same time, his extremities told a different story; despite their hot-headed 'tussle', his hands had already turned a weird shade of grey from the biting cold, and his eardrums ached from the constant icy wind.

As Anton's head moved slowly and steadily across the crater lake, Sean's anger, unconsummated, shifted its target from Anton and his glib attempt at foisting his unborn child onto him, to a pure self-directed rage for ever having agreed to meet Anton at this desolate spot. He tried to think what to say once Anton emerged from the water that would quell the bitter outrage welling up deep within him. Surely he could summon up a pithy, unequivocal speech that would give him the final word on the matter, or at least get one over on Anton? But he had absolutely no idea what outcome he needed from this ludicrous fiasco that Anton and Tess had fabricated. Strictly speaking, fornicated.

When Anton finally stepped out of the water, the tassels on his hat dripping and bedraggled, he shook himself like a dog and flapped around by the water's edge, trying to get dry. It was such a ridiculous sight, Sean had the sudden urge to laugh, which made him more angry.

'You should try it Sean, it's wonderful!' Anton enthused as he pulled his clothes back on.

'You're completely barking mad,' Sean muttered as he began to realise the futility of remonstrating with someone who didn't give a shit about anyone except themselves and for whom 'unexpected consequences' were never going to create much inconvenience or have any permanent impact.

Anton beamed benignly, as if they were just two old friends who'd hiked in a wholly civilised and responsible manner to see a famous crater. Once dressed, he pulled a small hip flask out of his backpack and slugged it.

'Did your camera survive to tell the tale?'

Sean looked down. The camera was still hanging around his neck, but there was a crack across the front of the lens, and the body was covered in dirt.

'No. It's fucked.'

'Just like you, mate. Shame. You shouldn't lose your temper so easily.'

Anton offered him the hip flask.

'You shouldn't be such a wanker!' Sean replied, then downed the rest of the brandy and hurled the empty hipflask into the middle of the crater lake.

As the sound of it splashing into the water combined with the echo of their childish insults returning from the far side of the crater, the surface of the lake went suddenly dark, as if a curtain had been drawn across Askja, bringing their whole shitshow to an abrupt end.

'Things are looking pretty ominous up there. Time to get our skates on,' Anton said, pointing to the bank of low black cloud making its way over the rim of the volcano.

'Yeah, we'd better make a move,' Sean agreed, getting to his feet and abandoning his shattered camera beside a pile of rocks. Perhaps he should set his grievances aside here too, make a fresh start. Anton seemed to have the knack of doing just that and moving on as if nothing had happened. What would you call that? Forgive and forget? Live and learn, perhaps. Or, more accurately: slash and burn. Whatever mantra Anton went by, it was borne of some bullshit mindset that only the very rich had access to. Whatever the truth of the matter, it seemed to Sean that the chill wind scouring the crater was intent on wiping the slate clean for both of them. He stood up, drew in a lungful of cold air through his mouth, which passed over the missing tooth and made his abscess ache. He dusted off his coat and jeans and started to scramble back up the side of the crater they'd just tumbled down. This was neither the right time nor the right place to deal adequately with Anton. Sean needed to hear Tess's side of the story first, before deciding how to serve Anton a nice, cold helping of revenge when they were back in England. That, he realised, would be the best way of dealing with this monstrous situation.

By the time they reached the crater rim, icy sleet was driving down at an oblique angle in thick white darts, reducing visibility to no more than a couple of metres. Battered into submission by the elements, neither of them could work out or remember which direction led back to the car park. It was taking a superhuman effort just to remain upright and think straight, and in the end the fierce arctic wind forced them to huddle together below the crater rim and wait for it to ease off a little. As the brandy from Anton's hipflask started to take effect, Sean scrambled along the perimeter of the crater, dimly aware that he'd lost all his bearings. Beginning to lose hope and wondering if they should just shelter somewhere and wait for the storm to pass, Sean came to a narrow gully which looked like a good place to take refuge from the wind and snow. He paused to assess the situation and steady his nerves, but Anton pushed right past him, huffing and puffing, and headed assertively into the gully.

Feeling physically and emotionally numb by this stage after the deadly combo of biting wind, bitter cold, too much anger and too little to drink, Sean watched Anton's colourful headgear disappear out of sight ahead of him. Snow was falling in thick clumps now, snagging on his eyebrows and burrowing its way inside the collar of his high-performance coat. He tugged the hood out from the bulge behind his neck and slid it over his head, pulling the toggles taut, leaving just a tiny portion of his face exposed to the elements. After descending a few metres into the gully, he stopped again, knee-deep in snow now, to catch his breath; either there must be less oxygen at this altitude or he wasn't as fit as he thought he was. He was certainly nowhere near as fit as Anton, who seemed able to cope in this challenging terrain without giving it a second thought. Sean brushed snowflakes off his eyelashes and tried to galvanise his legs, which were seizing up with the cold and the accumulated lactic acid.

A sudden, prolonged cry echoed up to him from somewhere further down the gully, and Sean peered blindly into the white void.

'Anton?' he barked.

There was no reply. Perhaps it was just one of those arctic foxes. Sean kept going, clambering now on his hands and knees as the gully became steeper. He could barely see anything through the heavy curtain of snowfall. Apart from the wind, everything had fallen silent and he suddenly felt entirely alone in this narrow gully, trapped between walls of volcanic rock, with no idea which way he was facing and unsure if there was even a way through up ahead. Reaching into his pocket and wishing he had thought to bring his own hipflask of brandy, he pulled out his phone to see where the compass was pointing, but the magnetism in the rocks all around him was making the app malfunction, and there was no way of knowing which way pointed north.

Sean stood still, his heart beating so rapidly it felt as if it was about to burst through his ribcage. He tried to calm his breathing. The cold air in his larynx hurt as he gulped it down. He felt sure that at any moment, he would hear Anton's voice shouting encouragement to him from above. He yelled his name again and again, even tried to text him, but of course there was no signal.

When Anton failed to respond or reappear, he began to suspect he'd found his way to the rangers' station in Dreki and the smug bastard was sitting right now in a warm cabin, sipping hot chocolate. Or else Anton had managed to retrace his steps back to his sports car and the lucky bastard was already on his way back to Djúpivogur, cursing his pathetic, hotheaded companion for yet another violent encounter and writing off the whole 'Mad Quest' as a bad trip.

Triggered by either prospect, Sean's anger was making his muscles twitch involuntarily as he reached the pitiful conclusion that he'd been abandoned by everyone in his life and left to die in this ridiculous barren wilderness. If he'd come better prepared, with things like ropes and rations and survival blankets, he could have easily contended with this predicament by holing up and keeping warm until someone found him. Lacking these mountaineering basics, his ego made it all Anton's fault and insisted that his main objective now was simply to get out alive. Especially since it would be dark soon. Even now, deep in this desolate gully, the snow had already taken on a bluish hue and Sean's core temperature was dropping rapidly. Any minute now he would go into shock or hypothermia or something. Because while his coat was keeping his top half warm, the rest of his clothes were completely unsuitable for these sub-arctic conditions.

Sean edged forwards a few more metres, the snow banking up against his thighs. He kept yelling Anton's name, but as the minutes passed, there was less and less conviction in his voice. Just as he was about to give up, he caught a glimpse of something tinged with colour trapped in a narrow gap in the rocks over to his right. He leaned out as far as he could, gripping the rockface with his left hand and reaching down into the gap until his right shoulder was almost wedged tight.

Fumbling around, his fingers made contact with something woollen and when he pulled it out, Sean found he was holding Anton's Peruvian hat, stiff with snow and ice. He pushed his shoulder back into the gap, convinced he would find the man it belonged to, but the only other thing that lay within his grasp was hard and made of plastic. It turned out to be Anton's yellow satellite phone, and in the fading light, Sean mustered enough strength and common sense to phone Sigga before hypothermia got the better of him and he passed out.

43

Compared to their much newer SUV, Sigga's old Land Rover was quite primitive, a farm vehicle with no heating, built for rough outdoor work. She drove in tense silence, but Olly found her thoughts so noisy, he put on his headphones and turned the volume up full, listening to Sol's favourite song on repeat, his mind sinking into a dark, rhythmic morass. It was the same track he'd played on that first day on the road, which gave the music extra significance; Olly felt that if he played it over and over, the sound waves would somehow reach his father and they would be miraculously reunited.

As Sigga turned off the highway onto a dirt track, Olly could feel the Land Rover's eagerness to measure up to the task at hand, matched by its driver's grim determination. She paused to check the weather app on her phone and take a quick swig of coffee from her insulated mug before continuing.

'Want some, Olly?' She asked, offering him the mug. He took off his headphones.

'No thanks, I've got my water.'

'Have you driven on any of these unpaved roads with your dad?'

'Nope.'

'They follow Iceland's old herding routes through what it known as Europe's last true wilderness. Rumour has it, the F26 got its name Sprengisandur meaning 'flog to death' because that's what you had to do to your horse if you were to have any chance of making it across the Highlands before the horse died of starvation and exhaustion.'

'I'd rather be in your Land Rover than riding a horse.'

'Exactly.'

Sigga changed down into a lower gear as they came to a ford, approaching the river at an angle to cross the churning rapids in a wide, practised curve before mounting the opposite bank. Olly looked out of his window at the glacial water, feeling it jostle the vehicle as it rushed past and he had a flashback of that awful moment when Baldur's Volvo swerved and rolled off the road. He still couldn't believe that they'd all survived and that he'd managed to get Baldur to hospital in that thing.

'Have you ever had to rescue someone in the Highlands before?' Olly asked quietly.

'Put it this way, this won't be the first time I've got your father out of a tight spot,' Sigga said, shaking her head.

'When was the last time?'

'In Indonesia, when he'd ventured too close to a volcano. He was assigned to a bunch of volcanologists on a scientific expedition to photograph the lava flows at Mount Tambora, but he got a little cocky and ended up being rescued by yours truly. Your dad was quite shaken up by the whole experience, just like when I sent him to photograph some sixteen-year-old war veterans.'

Olly couldn't remember his father ever telling him either of those stories.

'What happened in Indonesia?'

'Tambora belched out a load of poisonous gas while they were up there, and they all nearly died of smoke inhalation. I eventually got the emergency services to come and your dad ended up in hospital on a ventilator for a week. I think he lost his camera that time too.'

'I don't care about his camera, I just want to find my dad.'

'Of course you do, sweetheart, and of course we will. Don't you worry.' But there was something about the way Sigga said it that made Olly worry more.

'Anyway, let's not talk about your father, let's talk about you. It seems like you've been through quite a lot recently. But what doesn't break us only makes us stronger, that's what I always say. What are your plans for this gap year of yours?'

'It's not a gap year, really. I mean, I didn't choose to have one, but when I didn't get into uni, Mum said I should wait a year and reapply.'

'Well, it's a gap of sorts, whichever way you look at it. How do you plan to fill it?'

Sigga swerved round a large boulder that lay in their path, and Olly grabbed at the dashboard to steady himself.

'I'm not sure. Get a job, I suppose.'

'What kind of job would you like to do?'

They were bumping along over a particularly rocky section of track now, and Olly's voice had a strange fake-sounding shudder to it.

'I dunno. A job where I'm, like, helping people, maybe. And that gives me time to start my band.'

There it was again, that vague aspiration he'd expressed to her the first day in Húsavík.

Olly didn't want to pursue this conversation any further, so he changed the subject to something else that had been playing on his mind.

'Will Roman get better? I mean, his kidneys?'

'He won't have to be on dialysis forever, so long as someone comes up as a match for a kidney transplant. But there's a long waiting list at the moment. Kids usually get prioritised, but to be honest Roman might be waiting a while. The good news is, they've made a breakthrough with making synthetic kidneys, so that could be Roman's ticket to a long, healthy life.'

'Can't his Mum give him one her kidneys?'

'Usually that's an option, yes, but Katla's got a weird blood condition, so they're not compatible. And of course his father is er, as you know...'

Dead.

Olly completed Sigga's sentence in his head, saying the word she couldn't or wouldn't say, either because she didn't want to acknowledge the full extent of her grandson's difficult family circumstances or perhaps because Olly's own father was currently missing in action. He took Roman's spaceman figure out of his parka pocket and stared at its face, the painted features mimicking his own blank, searching expression.

'I love Roman.'

Olly wanted to say out loud that he loved his dad too, but the words wouldn't come.

'Don't we all; he's such a sweetheart. You know Olly, one thing you might want to consider is working for a kidney disease charity. There are lots of them; I can give you a list if you like. In fact, I can put you in touch with a very nice young woman who works for one based in London.' She glanced sideways at him to gauge whether or not this suggestion resonated.

'That's a cool idea. Thanks, I'll think about it.'

'Or what about working for an organisation that helps people with addiction problems?' Sigga asked, slowly segueing onto the other topic she wanted to bring up. This time Olly glanced sideways at her and then trained his eyes back on the strange square outline of the mountain in the distance.

'I don't have an addiction. I'm just suffering from depression,' Olly said guardedly.

'I know, Olly, sorry, that's not at all what I meant. You're going to be fine; it's your father I'm worried about. Has his drinking got a lot worse? You can tell me.'

'He stopped for a few days. After he saw the dentist. But he started again when we got to Akureyri. It's not the first time he's hit one of us. Mums thinks he doesn't know how to stop. And he outright refuses to join one of those programmes.'

'I thought as much. Goodness me Olly, adults do make a mess of things sometimes, don't they? It's a wonder your parents managed to conceive at all,' Sigga mused.

Olly went red and put his hood up.

'How do you feel about having a baby brother or sister?'

'It's probably a bit late now. And a bit fucked up.'

Sigga raised her eyebrows at his choice of words.

'I see. For you or for your parents?'

'For Anton.'

Sigga let out a muted gasp.

'Oh. Is there something I'm missing here?'

'Yeah, I reckon the baby might be his.'

Uttering this statement out loud was the first time Olly had acknowledged this awkward situation. Not long before this trip, he'd seen a pregnancy kit in the bathroom cabinet at home, and began to formulate his own theory.

Sigga pursed her lips and pressed her foot down on the accelerator to make the old Land Rover go a little faster. Olly stared through the icy windscreen, remembering a particular evening a couple of weeks ago when his dad was out and Anton came round to their flat and sat on the kitchen stool, but that time, instead of Anton making Olly's mother laugh, she did all the talking and ended up in tears. Olly, alarmed by the sound of his mother crying, crept out of his room and listened to their conversation behind the kitchen door. Anton kept saying, "Well we don't know for sure, do we, Tess?" and when she didn't reply, he said, "You could get rid of it, sweetheart."

'Does your dad know it's not his baby?'

'I've got no idea. But he did give Anton a black eye.'

Olly could feel a familiar wall of frustration building inside him, one he often erected to fend off his parents' inability to communicate with each other, to avoid being used as the go-between, shuttling back and forth across their pathetic marital no man's land. And he was definitely not going to get caught in the fallout anymore. Because when he took the decision to drink the thousand-year-old glacier water at the lagoon, he'd effectively made himself a promise not to play this role anymore. If there were gaps in their communication, it was his parents' business to sort them out. Just as his communication gap with Sol was something that only he and Sol could put right.

44

Snow was clogging up the windscreen wipers faster than they could swipe it away by the time they reached Dreki in the Land Rover, and when Olly opened his door, the wind nearly ripped it out of his hands, so he closed it again and remained in the passenger seat. Sigga got out, advising Olly to wait in the car while she went to speak to the ranger, and then she disappeared into the whiteness.

After waiting half an hour or more, Olly couldn't bear it any longer and he finally got out. He was in the middle of a blizzard in the middle of Iceland in the middle of a family emergency and he had to do something. He could feel the moisture in his eyes and nose instantly forming into icicles, and his feet felt like they weren't properly attached to his body. Telling himself that he was just going to look for somewhere warmer than Sigga's draughty vehicle, Olly zipped up his parka and headed in the direction she had gone, towards the only source of light he could see, which he assumed was the ranger's cabin. Parked near the cabin, he spotted a red sports car just like Anton's, covered in snow and mud. As he battled against the wind towards it, he could hear barking coming from somewhere, and realised it was inside the vehicle. He cleared away the snow from a side window and cupped his hands against it to peer inside. Apollo started pawing at the glass and turning in excited circles on the seat when he saw it was Olly.

'Now I know why you didn't come to say goodbye, Apollo!' Olly whispered. He yanked the door handle, but it was iced shut. The one on the driver's side was too. Eventually, after some persuasion, the tailgate gave way and Apollo leapt out, barking at Olly and wagging

his tail excitedly. He knelt down and murmured into the animal's ear.
'Apollo, my Dad is missing! You've got to help me find him.'

45

When Sean regained consciousness, he had no idea where he was and he could scarcely move any part of his anatomy. He had lost all track of time and most of his body heat. All he knew was that, on top of the extreme weather conditions, he was suffering from lack of sleep, lack of food and lack of water. As his body grappled with these physical issues, a single thought popped into his mind: Anton. Where was Anton? What had happened? Was he injured? Was he trapped? Was he even alive? And if he wasn't, was it Sean's fault?

Sean had forgotten he was holding Anton's woolly hat until he heard barking and felt a small creature brush against his legs and start tugging it out of his hands. Thinking he must be hallucinating, he desperately clung onto this one remaining shred of reality, believing that if he let go of the hat, he'd lost his friend Anton for good. This notion triggered the cynical part of his brain to start querying the precise nature of Sean's relationship to a man who was most likely now a frozen corpse: was Anton a friend? If so, in what sense was he a friend? A man who openly admits to sleeping with your wife, who got her pregnant no less, who is the sole reason you are in this horrendous situation, half-dead yourself. What friend would put you through suffering like this?

Sean let go of the hat.

Apollo ran off carrying it in his mouth, heading back the way he'd come. Sean followed, stiffly and blindly after the dog, hardly knowing what he was doing, just responding instinctively to any sign of life. And that's when he heard it: the sound of his son's voice, cutting through the arctic air with its pure, razor-fine vibration. By now completely delirious, Sean let himself be carried along by this precious wave of sound.

46

The dog returned to Olly's side with something in its mouth. He bent down to see what Apollo had found, but didn't recognise the strange knitted hat. Nevertheless, Apollo was barking excitedly as if trying to communicate the significance of his discovery, so when he trotted off again into the blizzard, Olly shoved the hat in his pocket and blundered along after him.

Sigga and the wooden hut had long since disappeared in the almost total white-out, and were it not for Apollo's barks, Olly wouldn't have had a clue which way to go. With every small step he took, he was terrified of a ravine swallowing him whole, because wasn't that what his dad said had happened to Anton? Perhaps his father had fallen into one too, while he was searching for Anton. Was his dad lying unconscious somewhere up here, having hit his head like Baldur? Olly realised he was more terrified of finding his dad's lifeless body than he was of risking his own existence in this uncompromising wilderness. And that made him determined to keep going.

Teeth chattering louder than the whistling wind, Olly edged his way forwards, trying to imagine the trail of scent Apollo had latched onto. In an effort to focus and keep his spirits up, Olly thought of Sol's words of encouragement, and suddenly felt inspired to sing. He managed only one note, and held onto it for as long as he could before his icy lungs were screaming for mercy.

47

After Sean lost track of the animal in the blizzard, there was only one thing left for him to cling onto for dear life: the sound of Olly's voice. It tore through him like a knife, the pain so visceral, so overwhelming, yet so beautiful. He wanted to cry but he couldn't. He wanted to hold his son, but he could barely hold himself upright, and began to wonder if he was even of this world, since his skin could no longer register sensory information and when Olly's singing faded to silence, he felt like his brain and body were shutting down.

In a final effort to stay conscious, he peered into the void and could dimly make out a faint red circle of hope in the darkening white wilderness. Lacking any other bearings, it seemed like a target he should be aiming for.

As Sean tried to get closer to the red target, but it kept moving away, as if it was attached to something mobile or alive. Lurching himself towards this apparition, he cried out and fell to his knees.

48

Olly felt something lunge at him from behind. An icy grip encircled both his ankles and he heard a piercing cry that reached inside him and squeezed his heart so hard, it felt like it would stop beating.

When Olly bent down and tried to loosen the vice-like hold around his ankles, his hands made contact with another human being. Apollo let out a single bark and ran off, leaving Olly struggling to heave the barely conscious human onto their feet. He managed to hook one shoulder under their arm and somehow hoist them upright.

'Steady, I've got you now,' Olly said, panting from the effort of supporting the person's whole body weight.

'Is that you, Mr Midas?' The person asked in a hoarse whisper.

'Dad?' whispered Olly, hardly daring to believe he'd found his father.

49

The air ambulance shimmied down onto the packed snow outside the ranger's cabin. Under different circumstances, Olly would have really enjoyed the whole spectacle of a helicopter rescue mission, but he was too exhausted and anyway the rotating blades threw up so much icy snow it was impossible to watch. Instead, Sigga and Olly helped Sean climb aboard, his arms and legs shaking like jelly, and the paramedics insisted that Olly got in too. Sigga leaned into the helicopter cabin, handed Olly a large envelope and tucked blankets around the two of them.

'You take care of your dad now, Olly. And Sean Mackie, I hope you know how lucky you are to have such a courageous, caring, incredible son. You'd better damn well get help, get sober and make amends before Tess's next child is born.'

She ducked under the blades and walked back to where the Ranger was standing with Apollo. Moments later, the helicopter rose up into the swirling whiteness over Askja and swept away. Somewhere below them, lost in a precipitous, windswept gully, was Anton's body. After hours of search and rescue, the paramedics had deemed him a lost cause, another tragic fatality, the inevitable consequence of foolhardy tourists who underestimate the power and majesty of the Icelandic Highlands.

Olly and Sean leaned against each other, shattered, dazed and relieved, no energy left to even think about Anton and everything else that had happened. The scuttering of the helicopter lulled them both into a fitful sleep as they skimmed over the endless pitch-black wilderness on the journey back to Reykjavík.

50

Olly had been sitting for hours by his dad's bedside, putting off leaving. The doctors were keeping Sean in hospital overnight to monitor his hypothermia, treat his damaged liver and manage his alcohol withdrawal symptoms. He was shaking less now, but his pulse was still very slow and his blood pressure weak. So he was hooked up to a drip and prescribed various types of medication with complicated names. The doctors also insisted on checking Olly over, but thankfully he didn't need any treatment and could go home.

He explained to the nurses that he didn't live in Iceland and didn't have anywhere to stay in Reykjavík, but they said since he was eighteen and therefore an adult, they could not let him stay overnight on the ward. Seeing his look of dismay, one of the nurses gave him the address of a youth hostel downtown.

'Right, I'd better go now Dad, see you tomorrow.'

'Don't leave just yet.' Sean reached out and caught his son's wrist, his hand and voice both shaky. 'I'm going to make it up to you, Olly, honest.'

'No need, Dad, just get help, like Sigga said. Mum's been telling you for years, but you wouldn't listen.'

'I am listening, Olly, and I will, I mean it. I'm going to those AA meetings and I'll do the whole twelve step thing, you'll see.'

'I hope so. It's better than being an angry mess that keeps lashing out. Anyway, what did Mum say when you spoke to her?' Olly asked.

'She said she's glad I'm still alive, so that's something.'

'Did you tell her about Anton?'

'I chickened out. I'll tell her tomorrow. She thinks…' Sean took a deep breath. 'She thinks the baby is his.'

Olly left a suitably shocked pause and thought about chickening out too, but something nudged him to speak up.

'I… I sort of knew. About the baby, I mean. I overheard Anton and Mum talking that night you were out at a client do with David.'

'So, are you telling me you all knew she was pregnant and were deliberately keeping me in the dark about it?'

'Come on Dad! Don't be paranoid; it wasn't like that. You need to get some rest.'

Olly patted his dad's hand and when he looked up, he saw that Sean was crying.

'Mum wasn't planning to keep the baby, Olly, that's why she hadn't told me, but after what's happened, I… I think she should go ahead and have it.'

'You do? Why?'

Everything came out in an incoherent wail.

'I don't know Olly, I feel terrible about what happened to Anton, and call it what you like, maybe it's just my way of dealing with the guilt, but I do feel for Anton. And the baby. I don't care whose it is; I just want Tess and me to bring your baby brother or sister into the world. We need to take care of the little mite, whoever the father is. Don't you think?'

Olly patted his dad's arm. He was so tired he hadn't got a clue what to make of it all.

'I think you need to talk it over properly with Mum before you make a decision. Look, I've got to go now, Dad. Love you.'

'I love you too, son. I'm sorry for messing up, and for everything you've had to deal with on this trip. I know I'm a fairly useless parent, but Sigga is right: somehow, I've managed to produce a very capable son. Thank you for going with her to look for me.'

'Sigga told me she had to bail you out once before in Indonesia, so you owe her big time now. Anyway, we didn't come to look for you, Dad. We came to save you.'

51

Olly stuck his hands in his parka pockets and walked out of the hospital in a daze. He could feel Roman's spaceman in one pocket and the knitted hat Apollo found in the other and headed for the bus stop to wait for a bus to the city centre. When it arrived, he panicked for a moment, thinking he had no money to pay for his fare, then remembered that in the envelope Sigga had given him before the helicopter flew away was some emergency cash and their two passports. Olly was still amazed at how she had the foresight to bring them with her in the Land Rover. Sitting on the bus, it suddenly occurred to him that their belongings were still in Húsavík, so he sent Sigga a text to ask if she could pack them up and send them back to the UK. Within half a minute she'd replied.

> *Don't worry, Olly, I've already done it. And the ranger is sorting out your SUV. There wasn't enough fuel in the tank to drive it back to Reykjavík so there will probably be a fairly hefty fine, but to give him credit, even though your dad never planned to take your hire car into the Highlands, at least he'd taken the precaution of asking them to put snow studs on the tyres.*

Olly wanted to text her back with a heartfelt thank you, but his phone promptly died. He wondered what would happen to Anton's red sports car, which was probably buried in snow by now back in Dreki.

Starving, Olly found the bus had dropped him right near the cafe his dad had taken him to over a week ago, so he decided to get something to eat there. Then he walked to the youth hostel downtown and booked himself a bed in a dorm for a couple of nights. Having borrowed a phone charger from the guy in the bunk opposite, he lay on his back, waiting for it to come back to life.

Above all, he was desperate for there to be a message from Sol waiting for him. He felt he truly deserved it after all he'd been through. But there was just one text waiting for him from Sigga, with a video of Roman greeting Apollo when they arrived back home in the Land Rover. He texted them back with a spaceman emoji, then rolled over on his side to call home.

'Mum? It's me.'

'Hey, you. Are you OK? Are you still at the hospital?'

'No, I'm at a youth hostel downtown. They wouldn't let me stay with Dad.'

'Look who's sounding all grown up! Is it clean?'

'Yes, Mum, it's clean. They even sell toothbrushes in a machine in the hallway.'

'I've been worried to death about you. Both of you. How are you feeling?'

'I'm fine. And the doctors reckon Dad'll be able to fly home in a couple of days.'

'Good, well you get some rest now, darling, and call me in the morning. Your father and I have put you through an awful lot. You must be shattered.'

'Will do. I am pretty tired. Love you, Mum.'

Olly hung up. He slipped off his boots and his outer layers and climbed into bed in his T-shirt and underwear. There was way too much to think about and none of it was in any way positive, and yet for some reason he felt happy. Happy that he was going to wake up tomorrow and be the one in the driving seat, so to speak, in control of his own destiny. Or maybe, just happy in the knowledge that he was through the worst of it now, whatever 'it' was.

He stood Roman's spaceman up on the shelf beside his bunk and turned out the light.

'Mission accomplished,' he murmured in the dark.

52

Olly showered, dressed and left the hostel to wander up the main street, Laugavegur. Halfway along, the pedestrianised street split in two, the right-hand part becoming 'Rainbow Street', the tarmac painted in wide bands of colour. He stopped to go in a little cafe called 'Eldur og Ís', which the tattooed girl on the serving counter told him meant 'Fire and Ice'. At her suggestion, he ordered himself the house speciality, a 'fire and ice' smoothie, and sat in the window to watch people walking past outside. It struck him how everyone was calmly getting on with their life, making choices that would shape today, tomorrow, next month, next year, and lead them somewhere new. Maybe it was time he did that too. Despite everything that had gone wrong on this trip, it had left Olly feeling less depressed and more confident. Because if he could be brave enough to sing at an open mic, rescue his friends from a car crash, get over being beaten up by his dad, and then save his parent from dying in an arctic blizzard, he could probably get through anything life chose to throw at him, so long as he faced it head on and made the most of everything.

'Takk. What do I owe you?' Olly asked, getting ready to leave. He paused, an idea taking shape in his mind. 'Do you mind me asking, where did you get your tattoos done?'

'A little studio called Obsession near the cathedral. It's further along Rainbow Street on the right.'

After Olly had located the tattoo studio, he continued up the hill towards the cathedral, drawn to its strange, tapering spire. It looked like the space shuttle used for the Apollo missions. He bought a postcard of it from a souvenir shop to send to Roman, then asked the shopkeeper the best way to get to the hospital. He was just looking up bus times on his phone when he got an alert from the stock image company Baldur had recommended, where Olly had sent his Northern Lights photos a few days ago while they were in Húsavík. He opened the message, and was amazed to discover that someone in America had bought the rights to his entire set of high-res images. Olly looked at the figure and laughed out loud. He had just earned himself a thousand quid!

Buzzing, he suddenly stopped in the midst of all the shoppers and tourists, because he knew what he would buy with the money: a new camera for his dad, to replace the one he'd lost in the Highlands.

Later, when Olly pushed open the door to the hospital ward, he saw for the first time how vulnerable and unwell Sean looked, lying in his hospital bed with an identity bracelet around his wrist and a saline drip going into his arm. For the first time, Olly realised that despite all the bluster, his father had no idea how to be his best self, let alone how to teach his son what it took either. Is that what made his dad act so critical and judgemental all the time? Was it because of his own insecurity and uncertainty? Is that what had turned him into a drinker? Or, as his Mum preferred to call it, a functioning alcoholic. All these years, Sean had managed to hold down a job, provide for his family, and as far as Olly knew, before this trip, had only ever got into one punch-up with Anton, and that was years ago. Twice now, if he counted the black eye his dad gave Anton last week. It was not as if Sean and Anton got violent over nothing; both times it was over Olly's mother, because they both loved her and didn't want to share her. Olly walked slowly over to his dad's bed.

'Hey Mr Midas, how's it going?' His dad's face brightened into a half-smile.

'I'm OK, how about you?' Olly leaned over the bed to give his father a hug and then pulled away, realising this kind of show of affection wasn't normal for them. They made eye contact instead and Olly poured his father a beaker of water. When Sean took a sip, it reminded Olly of the moment he'd drunk the beaker of thousand-year-old water at the glacial lagoon. It seemed a lifetime ago.

'I earned a grand today, Dad.'

'What? A thousand pounds?'

'Yeah. Someone bought all those photos I took of the Northern Lights.'

'Amazing. How come?'

'I uploaded them to a stock image website while we were staying at Sigga's house.'

'That's fantastic Olly. What about a cut for your old man, since you stole my camera to take them?'

Judging by the crushed look on his son's face, Sean realised he'd said the wrong thing. Again. But before he could apologise, Olly reached inside the pocket of his parka and pulled something out.

'I've got something I want to give you, Dad. Apollo found it on the mountain right before I found you. I know it's not your style, but it's good quality, hand-knitted probably. Someone must have dropped it. It's kind of like a souvenir of our whole adventure, don't you think?'

As soon as Olly gave him Anton's Peruvian hat, tears started rolling down Sean's cheeks, which turned into sobs. They kept welling up from a chamber somewhere deep inside his chest, and there was nothing he could do to stop them flowing. It felt like a lifetime of tears had been locked away, frozen solid inside him and somehow, right at this moment, here in Iceland, he had found a way to let them thaw. Perhaps it was the still too-fresh memory of Anton's untimely death – or his newfound admiration for his son – that had broken down the barriers and enabled it to happen. Whatever the reason, it felt like a blessed relief.

Olly was taken aback by his father's tearful reaction to his impromptu gift, and looked around to see if he could summon one of the nurses to help. Maybe his father was in worse shape than he realised. The doctors had said they wanted to keep him in for another night, to run more blood tests and give him more time to dry out. They didn't use the words 'cold turkey' but Olly guessed that's what they meant. He offered his father a tissue from the box beside his bed. His dad kept stroking the hat and running its purple and green tassels through his fingers, as if it was a long-lost friend. Finally, he cleared his throat to speak.

'This is… oh, get a grip Sean! This was… Anton's hat,' he gulped.

'Oh, wow! I didn't know…' was all Olly could reply.

They both stared at the hat for ages, saying nothing. Then Sean announced solemnly that he needed to call Tess.

'Are you going to tell her about Anton, Dad?'

'I have to. She needs to know. She's carrying his child.'

Olly nodded and started to pull the curtain around his dad's bed.

'Do you want me to stay with you while you call her?'
'No thanks Olly, I'll be fine. You go now.'

53

It was going dark when Olly emerged from the hospital, and there was a sprinkling of snow on the ground. But the cold night air was a welcome relief after all the emotion and stuffiness of the ward, and he decided to clear his head by walking all the way back to the hostel.

As he strode along the pavement next to the two-lane highway, he recognised a car park fringed with shops and take-away restaurants as the place where they'd rented their SUV on the first day. He paused and peered across the empty tarmac at the guitar shop where he'd photographed the poster for The Midas Rooms' open mic night. The lights were on and it still looked open. He headed across and pushed open the door, stomping the snow off his boots.

'Can I help you?' someone in a faded tour T-shirt asked.

'Just looking,' Olly said, and began a clockwise inspection of their impressive wall-mounted array of electric guitars. He stopped in front of a beautiful flame-red one, just like the Mayones guitar he and Sol had been looking at online. The neck was inlaid with a mother-of-pearl sun, its rays projecting in all directions. He lifted the guitar down from the wall carefully.

'It's a custom build,' the shop assistant said, 'If you'd like to give it a try, we have a booth over there.' He pointed at a small, glazed cabin in the corner.

'Thanks.'

Olly slid open the door and stepped into a tiny aquarium-like space with the red guitar. There was an amp inside with a couple of pedals attached to it, and he felt the surge of excitement as he plugged in the instrument and its edgy, metallic voice filled the space. Perching on the amp, he tuned the guitar, then plucked his way slowly through the new song that had been building in his mind on the way back to Reykjavík in the helicopter. It had no title as yet, but encoded in its DNA was the feeling of being set free, of having your whole life ahead of you, of being on an open road. Olly began to add a vocal line, softly and hesitantly at first, and then as he sensed its strong connection to the underlying chords, he felt himself opening up, as if his chest was full of buried treasure, and he was seeing it glitter for the very first time.

Someone tapped on the window and broke Olly's concentration. He looked round, a little startled, to see a man in his late thirties wearing big red glasses giving him a thumbs up. Olly slid the booth door open a couple of inches.

'Sounds great, what you're playing. Who wrote it?'

'I did. Well, technically, it's not been written down yet.'

'Have you written other songs?'

'A couple, yeah.'

'Amazing. Listen, when you're ready to record an album, let me know, I'd be interested in producing it.'

The man posted his business card through the gap.

Olly read the name printed on the front: Grímur Guðmundsson. Underneath it said in English, 'Music Producer'.

'Do you have a sister called Þórhildur?'

Grímur looked somewhat surprised and nodded.

'I met her and Baldur in Akureyri. We were on our way to see you when we had an accident in Baldur's car.'

'Aha! So, you must be the famous Al McKee? Þórhildur told me all about this incredible young man from England who came to their rescue and got Baldur to hospital. I gather you're the new owner of my orange effects pedal?'

'Thanks, yeah that's me,' Olly admitted shyly. 'Actually, it's Ol. Ol Mackie. What a co-incidence meeting you!'

'In Iceland, there are no coincidences Ol, just specially-timed encounters. May I come in?'

Olly shifted the amp over to make way for Grímur in the booth, and they stood around discussing music and guitars and pedals until the shop assistant came to tell them the store was about to close.

'Can I offer you a lift to where you're staying, Ol, if I promise not to crash my car?'

Olly grinned, hanging the red guitar back on the wall display.

'Thanks, but I'll make my own way.'

'Promise to email me when you're ready to record something, won't you?'

'I promise,' Olly said, shaking Grímur's hand, 'It was great to finally meet you.'

54

'Shall I come and get you from the hospital, Dad?' Olly asked, but when his father declined his offer, he said, 'Well then, get an Uber and meet me on the corner of Rainbow Street and Laugavegur. I've got an idea for our last day in Iceland.'

'OK kiddo… Sorry, I mean, good thinking Olly.'

When Olly had finished his breakfast, he began sketching out his idea on a napkin in the hostel's lobby area, ready to show his dad. His Mum was always telling the story about how she met Sean on New Year's Day in 2001on a residential street in Kilburn a minute after midnight. They'd both left their respective New Year's Eve parties early and were heading back to the tube station, Sean feeling sorry for himself that yet again at the cusp of midnight he was without a partner and Tess having just walked out on her boyfriend. Olly had figured out this boyfriend must have been Anton.

His parents probably wouldn't have noticed each other, if it hadn't been for the fact that Tess's heel got stuck in a gap between the paving stones and Sean went over to help her. Ever since, 01/01/01 was the only anniversary they celebrated, instead of their wedding day or the day Sean proposed.

'So, what's the plan? Sean asked breathlessly when he met Olly outside Eldur og Ís. He felt a bit discombobulated: three nights in an overheated hospital ward being plied with various drugs and subjected to countless tests, then suddenly being discharged to find he had to come to terms with a parent-son role reversal. He listened to his son explain what he had in store for the final day of their ill-fated trip.

'First we're going to a place called Obsession, just up here,' Olly said, pointing.

'I've done far too much obsessing recently, Olly, do we have to?'

'This'll be worth it, Dad.'

The entrance to the tattoo parlour was off a small yard round the back, with a large flowing mural painted onto a corrugated tin wall. Once inside, Olly pulled out the paper napkin and spread it on the table in the reception area to explain the idea to his dad.

'So, about that tattoo on your bum.'

'You've brought me here because you want to get a tattoo?'

'No, not me. You, Dad. I thought you could surprise Mum – and also make it up to her – by getting it altered like this,' Olly said, pointing to a careful reworking of *METTE* into 'MET TESS 01/01/01'.

'That's very clever, Olly. But I don't know if I can stand the pain. I can still remember the last time, and that was eons ago.'

'You'll be doing it for Mum, for love, Dad. It won't hurt.'

'OK, but only if you get one done too.'

'Me? You'd let me? I don't think Mum would approve.'

'You're eighteen now, why not?' Sean was surprised to hear himself suggesting this, while simultaneously realising it wasn't his place any longer to give his son permission. Olly was his own man now, a fully grown adult.

'I hadn't thought about it,' Olly faltered, staring at the pin board where photos of all the previous clients' tattoos were displayed.

The tattoo artist appeared and ushered Sean into a brightly lit bay behind a curtain, leaving Olly alone in the reception area. His thoughts kept drifting back to the beautiful mother-of-pearl sun on the guitar he'd tried out the previous night, and that's when it suddenly came to him. If he couldn't have Sol, he could at least have a little tattoo of a sun done, to remember their relationship by. It would be just like when his dad got the 'Mette' tattoo because he was hopelessly in love. But Olly wasn't going to get the sun emblazoned on his butt. He was going to get it just above his belly button, on his solar plexus, right where Sol had planted their one and only kiss.

55

'No case?' the taxi driver asked them in a strong accent that wasn't Icelandic, mystified about how two tourists could have spent a fortnight in Iceland without a suitcase between them. Sean made no attempt at a reply and got in the back seat of the taxi. Olly shrugged and hopped into the front seat with his backpack.

'We've left all our baggage behind,' he told the man in Polish as they set off.

They drove south through the narrow streets of central Reykjavík and joined the highway to Keflavík. Before long, the houses and apartment buildings were replaced with an endless lava field, punctuated with glimpses of the sea to their right and the occasional shaft of sunlight glancing off the shiny road ahead.

'Nice to meet someone in Iceland who speak some Polish,' the taxi-driver enthused, beaming at Olly. 'Good trip?'

'In the end, yeah.'

Olly unzipped his parka and smiled. He was pleased that he'd managed to change their airline booking on his iPhone and get the last two seats on the evening flight back to Heathrow. He was also pleased that it left them enough time to take a dip in the Blue Lagoon on the way to the airport, because he remembered his dad insisting on the plane before they landed, 'you can't come to Iceland and not go there'. Olly had probably fobbed him off by saying he was totally against going in any outdoor pools, but today he was warming to the idea of relaxing with his dad in geothermal water. It seemed a very apt way to end this whole experience. Come to think of it, this trip had finally enabled Olly to put his swimming pool trauma behind him.

'Not far to the Blue Lagoon, Dad. You're very quiet, are you feeling OK?' he asked, glancing over his shoulder. Sean hadn't shown Olly the amended tattoo, nor had he said a word since they'd left the parlour. He seemed deep in thought, staring out of the window at the endless expanse of dark lava rolling past.

Olly's phone buzzed in his hand and when he turned it over, he saw he'd received a text alert from Icelandair informing him that their flight would be delayed by a few hours because the Geldingadalir volcano had just erupted.

It was the same one he'd seen on the front page of Sigga's newspaper, but Olly still wasn't sure where the volcano was, so he googled its location and discovered it was on the same peninsula as the airport and the Blue Lagoon. When they'd set out on this trip around Iceland, as far as Olly was concerned, there were only two things he was looking forward to, both of which his father had told him were highly unlikely: seeing the northern lights and getting close to an active volcano. Miraculously he'd ticked the first one off his list the night he borrowed his dad's camera and driven their hire car without permission. Now it seemed as though there was a chance he might fulfil the second one, right before their departure. Hadn't Sigga told him that his dad wasn't supposed to go up Mount Tambora in Indonesia, but he went anyway? Nor was Olly supposed to have got into trouble at the music festival with Sol, but it happened anyway. Just like Sean wasn't supposed to have gone into the Icelandic Highlands. But everything happens for a reason, right?

'Let's skip the Blue Lagoon, Dad,' Olly said suddenly.

'What?' Sean said, frowning.

'There's something more important that we need to do.'

Olly reached into his backpack and pulled out his dad's map of Iceland. He unfolded it on his lap and spotted a route that might work. A few miles further on, he asked the driver to make a detour onto a minor road which brought them to an impromptu car park in the middle of nowhere. Three other people, all carrying cameras with massive lenses, had just arrived and were getting out of their car. Olly felt like they'd all received a secret tip-off.

'Shame we haven't got your camera, Dad; we'll just have to make do with my iPhone,' he said, 'Come on, let's go!'

As they came over the crest of a hill, Sean finally saw why his son had wanted to stop here. In the distance, forking its way across the hillside, was a vivid orange river. Following the group of photographers, they walked towards the nearest tongue of bright orange lava, and Olly gasped as he felt its heat burning his cheeks from several hundred metres away. He took out his phone and started to take photographs, while Sean stood next to him with his hands in his pockets, watching the new liquid rock as it ran over the rutted surface of the last eruption, filling in all the gaps in its sluggish wake, healing over the wounded surface of this fragile volcanic landscape, remaking the land and inscribing its surface with a brand new topography.

Olly pictured the invisible contours of this mountainside changing by the moment, being rearranged by a molten substance that had come from somewhere deep in the earth's core, to cool right here into solid rock. Just like the melted glacier water he'd drunk, which had been trapped in an iceberg for a thousand years before finally melting and flowing freely, this molten rock had been trapped for millennia beneath the earth's surface and had now pushed its way up to freedom.

He zoomed in and filmed the exact moment when a stretch of molten lava started crusting over, turning from luminous orange to a deep blue-grey, its edge lacy and elastic, as it covered over everything that had come before. Olly's whole being was glowing with the heat and the feelings it was stirring up inside him. Perhaps it was all the geothermal energy going on around him, but at that moment he suddenly felt incredibly alive.

Turning to face Sean, for a brief moment Olly's eyes looked as if they too were glowing bright orange. His whole face was lit up, his expression jubilant and carefree. Sean felt a lump in his throat.

'This is so awesome, Dad! Thanks for bringing me to Iceland.'

Olly raised his right hand to high five his father, but instead of raising his own palm to meet it, Sean grabbed hold of Olly's hand and pulled his son towards him. It turned into an awkward kind of hug, but it felt warmer and more real than the heat from the volcano.

'I'm proud of who you are, Ol,' he said gruffly as Olly pulled away. Halfway back to the taxi, Sean stopped, took Anton's hat out of his pocket and put it on.

'We need a picture of the two of us, Olly. For posterity.'

'What, you want us to take a selfie with the volcano?' Olly laughed.

Olly held his phone at arm's length, and they posed with the volcano behind them, Sean wearing Anton's Peruvian hat and Olly with Roman's salt-dough medal around his neck.

'Finally, a father and son snap!' Tess replied when Olly texted the picture to his mum. And a few seconds later, she couldn't resist commenting on two things: his dad's awful choice of headgear and Olly's wonky fringe.

56

Several hours later, Olly closed the overhead locker, sat down and strapped himself into the aisle seat next to his father.

'I've let Mum know we're finally on our way,' he said nudging his father's elbow, but Sean was already fast asleep with his mouth open. Olly could see the empty space where his dad's bad tooth had been and took it to be a good sign that all the bad things were over. Maybe if the rifts in their relationships were on the mend, it somehow meant his silent prayer at the lagoon, when he drank the glacier water, had actually worked.

After draping his parka across his father's lap to keep him warm, Olly bent forwards to put his phone in the seat pocket and saw there was a text notification. His mother must have already replied. But when he checked, Olly let out a deep, contented sigh. Because it was not from Tess.

It simply said, 'I'm finally coming out, Sol xx.'

Thank you for reading this book. If you enjoyed it, please consider putting a review on Amazon or Goodreads, as this will help other readers to find my books and I'd really love to know what you thought of this story. You can also send me an email via my website if your school would be interested in arranging an author visit.

SARAH HOLDING

Before becoming a full-time author, Sarah was an architect,
a university professor and an urban development consultant.

She is married with three children and divides her time between
England and Japan, writing and looking after two old houses.
When she's not writing, Sarah loves reading, painting,
cooking, travelling, singing and playing jazz.

Her debut title, the best-selling middlegrade trilogy *SeaBEAN*,
now in its 4th edition, is being taught in schools
across the UK and around the world .

In addition to her two previous YA novels, *Chameleon* and *blackloop*,
Sarah has also published a poetry anthology, *How to Write a Poem*.
She regularly gives talks and creative writing workshops
in primary and secondary schools.

sarah-holding.com

twitter: @seaholding
instagram: @officialsarahholding
Sarah is also on Facebook, Goodreads and YouTube.